Call me an UBER!

A Novel by

LAUREN *"LUSH"* COLLIER

Written, Edited & Illustrated

By Lauren "*Lush*" Collier

DEDICATION AND THANKS

I would like to dedicate this book to all of my supporters and fans, thank you for believing in me and encouraging me to keep writing. Thank You for letting me be who I am, and to let me share my inner thoughts and wild imagination with you. I want to thank everyone who has purchased my poetry books, *Sundae Poetry* and *Passion Fruits*, I hope you will enjoy this book as well. To all of my readers stay tuned for much more to come! I love you all, Lush.

CONTENTS

Preface

It is 5:17 in the morning, so far Kacie is doing fairly well with timing. Her cab guy, Tyrone is on his way and Kacie and her overstuffed luggage are soon to be headed downstairs.

"Kacie! Kacie! I'm over here!" Tyrone, the cab driver shouts. She scurries her way to his minivan. "Oh my, god, Ty! Thank you so, so much for coming to my rescue at such the last minute," Kacie says. "I'd drop anything for you woman, but of course you know that," Tyrone says, tilting his shades from his eyes and gazing in her big hazel ones.

This man has had a thing for Kacie since they met back in April of 2013 at a grocery store not too far from her building. She had purchased a shit load of groceries that day, and as she struggled out of the store she heard someone yelling, "Taxi Cab!" Tyrone stood about 6'1", 200 lbs. He had a pretty, smooth cocoa colored complexion. He approached Kacie with his huge hand extended and introduced himself to her, and instantaneously began loading her bags into his minivan. "How far are you going, beautiful?" He asked her and smiled then hopped in the front seat directing him to her apartment building only a few blocks away. When he dropped her off he gave her his business card and said to call him anytime, no matter the distance. And that was the start of a new friendship, or as Kacie's home girl, Chelsea would say, "Friends with business and pleasure-ship."

CHAPTER 1

FLIGHT 291

"Final call for flight 291, flying into Chicago, Illinois!" Startles Kacie from the overhead loudspeakers. *Shit, that's me!* Kacie starts to pick up the pace. *What the hell, I thought we board in a fuckin' hour, no time for my iced coffee, nothing! Ugh!* Kacie finally arrives at her gate, gasping for air. "Woooo!" she lets out. "Excuse me, miss? I thought this flight boards at 7:30?" Kacie asks the flight attendant. "Um, no, Ma'am it takes off at 7:30, we boarded 30 minutes ago. Do you have your boarding pass?" Kacie hands her the boarding slip. The attendant scans her pass, "Okay! You're all set, hurry along now!" "Thank you, Misssss!" She shouts as she takes off faster than a track runner.

Kacie makes it to the entrance of the airplane where she is greeted by an overly ecstatic male flight attendant, named Adonis. "Welcome to Jet Blue Airlines, flight 291, as you can see the flight is not full, so please sit wherever you'd wish," says Adonis. "Wow, you guys really did some renovations to the inside, very nice. Umm, so you say I can sit anywhere, even in first class?" Kacie asks flashing a wide smile. "You absolutely can," he replies. "Oh thank you, thank you, thank you! You are the best!" She sings. The pilot announces that they will shortly be taking off and should arrive at their destination in one hour and forty-five minutes. Kacie finds an empty row of seats in first class and places her luggage in the overhead compartment.

She holds onto her purse and goodie bag filled with chocolate chip cookies, starbursts and a big bag of party mix. "Ahhh," Kacie sighs, as she plops down in her comfy seat.

Let's see what's on the menu for today, ooh spinach and cheese omelet, caesar salad with grilled chicken. French toast, and fresh fruit. Okay, now where is that alcohol menu…ah ha, here you are. Kacie picks up the drink menu and oohs and ahhs at the choices: merlot, red zinfandel, moscato, jack daniels, Patron, and vodka with cranberry juice. *So many selections, hmm, I'm gonna go with Patron, I wonder if they can make it a margarita.* "Adonis! Adonis!" She calls out. "Yes, beautiful?" He asks. "Hey, I know the flight is early and pretty short but I'm starved, and in need of a strong drink," she says chuckling. "Don't be shy, Hun what can I get you?" "Okay, great. May I please have the spinach and cheese omelet and the french toast, and from the drink menu I'll take the Patron on the rocks, wait, would it be possible to have a Patron margarita?" Please say yes, LOL." "Lol, sure, I think I can whip that up for you," says Adonis. "Thanks a million, sweetie," Kacie says batting her sexy eyes and handing him her credit card.

Oh, this is the life! Man, I sure do miss my baby, I so wish we could have taken this little trip together. I can't wait to call him and let him know how much I miss his fine, chocolaty ass, yum! Just thinkin' about him and the last time we fucked is making me hot!

Kacie is heading to Chicago for business, but plans to stop by her family's house in Wisconsin while there.

Kacie's drink arrives, she swirls it around with a tiny straw. "Oh, yes! Now this is perfect, just what I needed! Thank you, sweetie," Kacie says joyfully. "You're welcome…It's Kacie, right?" "Yes! I'm so sorry, where are my manners." "No worries, you were in quite a rush, now you enjoy that drink and I'll check on the entrée." Kacie reacted with a wink and charming smile. Several minutes later, Adonis returns with a piping hot plate. "Here you go, nice and hot," says Adonis. "Yummy, look at this food; looks marvelous," she says. "Yes it does, give me a holler when you've cleaned your plate, dear."

Boy, am I gonna take my time savoring every bite of this.

Kacie planned on checking her emails and reading a book for the duration of the flight, but that good ole food put her right to sleep.

The pilot announces overhead that they will be landing in 15 minutes. Adonis walks by and collects her plate and empty margarita glass as she continues to rest. "Adonis, your friend is knocked out huh?" Another flight attendant nudges him and says. "LOL, yes child, that good food put her to bed…or maybe it was the drink (giggles)," they both laugh. "Princess K!" Says Adonis while tapping Kacie on the shoulder, she instantly wakes up appearing slightly puzzled.

"Huh?" Kacie asks. "Time to wake up, babygirl we'll be landing soon." She wipes the drool from her mouth. "O.m.g, thank you, Hun I hadn't realized I fell asleep," says Kacie. Adonis smiles and starts to walk away. "Hey!" She shouts. "Yes, Love?" Adonis asks. "I just want to say thank you for your outstanding service throughout the flight." She starts to hand Adonis a 20 dollar bill, but he stops her. "Oh, Kacie you don't have to." "No, don't be silly, I insist," she says. Adonis accepts the 20 and gives Kacie a big hug and a kiss on the cheek, the two both smile, and Adonis heads toward his seat for landing.

"Whoa! That was kind of a rough landing, huh?" Kacie says in a frightening tone to the passenger in front of her. "Yeah, I'd say, thank God it wasn't any worse!" Replies the gentleman. "Welcome to Chicago, Illinois. Thank you for flying with Jet blue airlines, everyone please enjoy your trip!" The pilot announces. The passengers gather their belongings and make their way to the front of the plane for exit. Kacie finds her way to Adonis for one last thank you and to say farewell.

"Goodbye, my Love, and thanks again for everything! Smooches," Kacie says to Adonis puckering up her bodacious lips. Adonis catches her air kiss on his cheek and says, "Yes, farewell baby-girl! I hope you enjoy your stay!" "Thanks, I hope so too!" She yells as she strolls down the walkway.

Where is this driver, he should have been at the gate waiting for me! I have a meeting to be at in two hours and I need to freshen up!

Kacie's driver finally arrives at her gate, fifteen minutes later than scheduled. "Dude, what the hell?! I have somewhere very important to be!" Kacie shouts. "Ma'am, I understand that and I apologize, but you don't have to yell," says the driver. Kacie huffs and puffs but remains calm, "Whatever, just get my bags please," she directs him. The two walk off with a bit of tension in the air. Luckily for Kacie the driver, Ernie parked fairly close to the exit. Ernie opens the door of the cab for her and places her luggage in the trunk. He hops in the driver seat and types her destination in his GPS device. "Ms. Fuller, I am truly sorry for any inconvenience I may have caused you, I had a rough start this morning, though that is no excuse," says the driver hanging his head. "Well, we all have our days; I apologize for raising my voice a short while ago. I hope all is okay with you," Kacie replies. Ernie smirks at Kacie through his rearview mirror then buckles his seatbelt for their drive ahead.

"I Wanna be down" by Brandy blares thru the speakers. "Ooh! Turn that up, that's my jam!" Kacie tells the driver, he laughs and does as she requests. They both bump their heads to the song as Kacie sings along.

Kacie is a beautiful woman inside and out, but she can be a tad standoffish if she doesn't know you, or if you rub her wrong. She is well educated and talented with a Bachelor's degree in creative writing.

Her honey complexion is flawless, she has a full set of lips, amazing ass with a matching set of boobs. She stands at 5"5', 200 pounds; a full figured lady. She has no kids but hopes to have a big family one day.

After riding in the cab for fifteen minutes Kacie arrives at her hotel where she will be staying for the night. The hotel is enormous; Kacie is stunned by its magnitude and exquisiteness. "Wow! Now this is a hotel!" Kacie says aloud. "Ah, yes, this is a very popular hotel, Ms. Fuller; I assure you will love it here," says Ernie." "Great, 'cause I most definitely needed to get away for a little while, even though it's for business," says Kacie. Ernie opens the car door and assists her to the curb; he then removes her luggage out of the trunk. Kacie hands him a $100 bill, which included a generous tip. "Why thank you, Ma'am, I will put this tip to good use," Ernie says to Kacie with a jolly smile. "No, thank you for getting me here safe and sound, I truly appreciate it, and I hope your night goes better than your morning did." He thanks her and hops back in his vehicle.

"Ring! Ring! Ring!" Kacie's phone goes off.

Damn, I can't even step foot in my room before someone blows up my phone!

-"Hello!" says Kacie
-"Yo, baby wassup?" Says the caller.

-"Hey, baby I'm so sorry I didn't call when I landed, my driver was late so it threw me off a bit," says Kacie.

-"It's cool, lil' mama I'm missing you like crazy, yup, already, lol," says Dante', Kacie's boyfriend.

-"Ha-ha-ha, boo you crazy, but you know I miss you too. I'm just getting in my room; let me call you back in a few."

-"Okay, sexy I love you, and you better hit me back!"

-"I will boo you know that, I love you too, talk later, muah!" Kacie says and hangs up her cellphone.

"Ring! Ring! Ring!" Just several minutes later her phone rings again.

Really, are you serious?!

-"Hello! Kacie answers the phone annoyed.

-"Damn, somebody has jet lag, or just needs some fuckin' dick in their lives," says the female caller.

-"Lol, Chelsea you play way too much, wassup tho boo?"

-"I'm just checking on my bestie, making sure she had a safe flight, you could have called you know, got me and your boy all worried!"

- Kacie giggles and says, "D called your phone harassing you, huh?"

-"Yes, girl he does not play when it comes to his butter pecan queen. He had me all shook up 'cause I knew for sure he would've been the first to know that you landed safely."

"I know right, I was so damn tired that it slipped my mind. But, Chels I need to take a quick

nap before this big meeting, ok? Love you talk later,"
Kacie says.
-"Okay, baby mama love you back! Says Chelsea,
and they both hang up the phone. Kacie decides to
turn off her phone to avoid any further distractions.

*Damn, this is a sexy ass suite; my Job sure knows
how to hook a sister up.*

Kacie takes off all her clothes except for her bra and
panties, and hops in the king sized bed.

Ahhh, so, so nice… "Zzzzz"

"Beep! Beep! Beep!" Twenty-five minutes went by and
Kacie's alarm clock starts to go off.

Ugh! That time already?! My eyes are burning!
Kacie drags herself out of what seemed to be the
most comfortable bed in the world. She heads into the
bathroom to take a much needed shower. Ten
minutes later she is feeling fresh and new. She dries
off her body with a plush towel and blow dries her
long curly hair.

*No time to flat iron this bad boy, into a ponytail you
go.* Kacie lathers up every section of her body with a
sweet mango-butter body cream, and picks out a
classy, yet, stylish outfit. She steps into her maroon
panties, puts on her matching bra and starts to iron
her dress suit. Now that Kacie is all dressed and
ready for business she calls the concierge downstairs
for a cab number.

"Hi, may I have a cab number please?" Kacie asks the lady who answered the phone.
"Sure, I have a few," the lady says.
"Any will do," Kacie replies.
"Okay, here is the number for Magnificent Drives, (773) 444-2323"
"Great, thank you, Ma'am," says Kacie and hangs up the phone.

Kacie calls the cab number she was given and they arrive at the hotel ten minutes later.

"Right on time," Kacie says to the cab driver, a pretty, young Caucasian woman. The driver was already outside of the car with the door opened. "Hello, watch your head," she says to Kacie as she enters the cab. The driver goes back to her seat and Kacie immediately gives her the address for the business meeting. "Aren't you going to put that into your GPS?" she asks the driver. "No, I know my way around this town pretty well," the driver chicly says. "Oh okay, my bad," Kacie replies as she sits back in her seat, she then places her Bluetooth on her ear and makes a phone call.

-"Hey, Kay-kay baby!" The caller excitedly says.
-"Hi, mom! I'm just calling to let you know I'm safe, and I'm heading to my meeting now," Kacie says.
-"Okay, honey great, you know your dad and I were worried a bit, but we didn't want to pester you."

"Stop, Ma, it's no bother, tell dad I love him...let me go, I'll call you guys later."
"Okay, K I love you, and stay awake at that meeting!"
"I will, love you, talk later.
"Bye-bye, now," says Kacie's mother, Belinda.

Kacie hangs up the phone and texts Dante'.

Kacie- Hi, sexy face.
Dante'- My boo! Wassup, gorgeous?
Kacie- Heading to this meeting, was just thinkin' 'bout my man.
Dante'- Mmm, is that right? I'm thinkin' 'bout my lady too. I'ma hit you back tho, cutie I got some running around to do.
Kacie- Yea, aight, nigga don't act up!
Dante'- LOL, come on now, babe I'm too old to act up. Enjoy that meeting, love u!
Kacie- Love you back, baby boy. Don't text me; I'll hit you, no telling how long I'll be stuck in there.
Dante'- Copy.

   "We're here! The cab driver yells out.
"Okay, now that was fast," Kacie says.
"Told you I know my way around," replies the driver.
"Thank you, it's a round trip so I'll see you soon, well hopefully soon!" "Okay, no problem," says the driver, Alexis. Kacie hands her $40 and lets herself out of the cab. She waves to Alexis and makes her way to the large, historical looking building.

Wow! This place is beautiful, Kacie thought to herself as she walked through the automatic double doors. After admiring the décor and paintings, Kacie strolls over to the person at the greeter's desk.

"Hi, my name is Kacie Fuller, I'm here for a meeting with Dub Fashions," she says.
"Ah, yes, third floor, conference room 1," says the greeter. "Thank you, Ma'am which way are the elevators?" "Down the hall and to your left," says the concierge.

Kacie finds the elevators and rides it up to the 3rd floor. The floor is quiet but filled with a lot of people working at cubicles. She locates conference room 1 and knocks on the wooden doors.

"Knock! Knock!"
Someone from the inside opens the door.

"Yes?" Asks the guy in the conference room.
"Hi, I'm Kacie from-"
The gentleman stops her.
"Yes, I know where you're from, Ms. Fuller come on in," he says.
The room is empty besides the man who greeted her and a husky fella in suspenders.

"Ms. Fuller, welcome," says the husky man.
"Hello, nice to meet you, Sir," Kacie says.
"Mr. Trouser, you can call me Mr. Trouser. Have a seat, dear the others should be arriving soon. Would you like some coffee or tea? And there's bagels and pastries as well," he says.

Kacie has a sweet tooth so she doesn't hesitate to grab a bite or two. "Don't mind if I do," says Kacie. She pours herself some fresh, hot coffee from the canister and adds 2 lumps of sugar and a lot of cream. She then grabs an Everything bagel and smears vegetable cream cheese on it; thick like a bar of soap.

"Yum, everything looks delicious, thank you," Kacie says. "Thanks, we order from the best bakeries for our employees," Mr. Trouser tells Kacie.
"That's nice of you guys, I appreciate that," she says with a wide smile. Four more people start to enter the room, everyone is dressed to impress and the women in tall heels. Several minutes after that two more people arrive.
"Sorry we're late," one of the gentlemen states.
"No biggie, now let's get started," declares Mr. Trouser.

Mr. Smith, the man who greeted Kacie at the door brings out a projector screen. In front of everyone there's a laptop and a pen and pad.

"Hello, everyone welcome, we will be here for a few hours so please make yourself comfortable. Today you are here because you play an important role in this multi-million dollar company, Dub Fashions. Before we get started on today's presentation we would like to thank you all for your hard work, and dedication. My team and I have selected a few rewards that we felt would serve as a token of our appreciation.

The first reward is an all-inclusive trip for you and your family for 7 days/ 6 nights to anywhere you want to go in the world, I'm talking Paris, Dubai, um, India, wherever you want to go, you can go there. The second reward is a 2017 Lamborghini, no monthly car note and one year of free car washes and oil changes. And lastly, everyone will receive a bonus of $50,000.00 on their next paycheck.

Wow, that's a lot of good shit, but what's the catch?

"Excuse me, Mr. Smith, all of this sounds rather gracious, but what's the catch?" Asks one of the gentlemen. "Why does everything have to be a catch with you, Steve? Just be happy for this blessing they're offering to us," says a lady next to him. Steve rolls his eyes and repeats the question. "Well, um, all we require is a contract between Dub Fashions and its best teammates; you guys," says Mr. Smith. He then passes the contracts out to everyone.

Everyone examines their contract.

"Yea, umm, this won't work," says Kacie aloud. "Excuse me, Ms. Fuller, and why is that?" Asks Mr. Smith. "C'mon now, none of us in here are fools," she says. Mr. Trouser steps in and says, "Ms. Fuller would you mind elaborating? Because I can assure you we don't think of any of you as a fool." "Let me get this straight, you want us to sign a contract with you without any health benefits? You want us to work at your will?

And on top of that, there's no getting out of this seven year contract once it's signed. No retirement plan like 401K? Nothing, but a decent paycheck, and some gifts? Don't get me wrong I love all of that, but I need stability, and security. You have to come better than this! "Yeah, preach on sister!" Shouts one of the other women. Mr. Trouser takes a deep breath, "Let myself and Mr. Smith take a few minutes to go over the contract, you guys can take a quick break, we'll let you know when you can come back in.

The workers disperse.

I can't believe those motherfuckers would try to stick us in a shitty contract like that.

Ten minutes later everyone is called back in the conference room.

"Sorry if we may have upset a few of you, we do sincerely want the best for Dub Fashions, that's why we have decided to let Ms. Fuller go," said Mr. Smith (everyone's face looked stunned).
"Excuse me?! Kacie questions with a scrunched up face.

"Mr. Trouser and I feel that your attitude is disgusting and is causing a negative effect on the others." "Bull! Does anyone besides the "bosses" feel that way? She asks. Everyone's hand goes up. "Oh hell no! I've been busting my ass off for this company for the last five years, and you let me go because I speak my mind, and won't sell my soul by signing your bogus ass contract? Each and every one of you in this room…can kiss my yellow, wide, round ass!" "Ohhhh!" A guy in the room blurts out.

Kacie snatches up her belongings and storms out of the room. "Arghhh!" She lets out in frustration.

"Hello, Alexis please come and get me now before my ass gets sent to jail!" Kacie shout through the phone to her driver. "Oh my, be there in five!" Says Alexis frantically.

Exactly five minutes later Alexis pulls up to the building, and Kacie wastes no time getting in the car. They sat in silence for a few minutes until Kacie bursts out in a sob.

"Oh my, please don't cry, what's wrong, Ms. Fuller?" Alexis asks. "You can call me Kacie, and I'm so fed up right now! I just lost my fuckin' job. How am I supposed to survive now?" Replies Kacie. "You seem like a very smart woman, I'm sure you will figure things out," says Alexis. "You know what, you're right. Where's the closest bar; I need to take my mind off of this," Kacie pleads. "Well, that surely will do the trick! To the bar we go," says Alexis.

A few minutes later they pull up to a small, shabby sports bar. "I know it doesn't look like much, but I get frequent flyers here," Alexis proclaims. "As long as there's liquor inside I'm a happy camper. Would you like to join me?" Kacie asks. "Sorry, but I'll have to pass I have some runs to make, but enjoy and please be safe!" Alexis says.

"Aww, okay I will, nice meeting you, babe and wish me luck with everything." "You're in my prayers, Kacie, and it was a pleasure meeting you as well, take care now!" Alexis drives off and Kacie walks slothfully to the sports bar.

Kacie finds a seat at the bar and orders a double shot of Hennessey, and some buffalo wings.

   "Extra blue cheese please!" She shouts to the server as she walks off to put her order in. The server replied with her thumbs up. Kacie twiddles with her phone pondering who she shall call first to let off some steam. Before she could decide her phone rings.

-"Hello?" Says Kacie
-"Hi, beautiful how are you?" Asks the male caller
-"Not so great, Ty," she replies
-"Sorry to hear, what's going on?"
-"I got fired today, blew my whole fuckin' mind."
-"Damn, K that's crazy. What are you gonna do now?"
-"I'll figure shit out when I get back to NY, gonna go see my aunt and cousins later tonight."
-"Okay, dear well you know if you need anything, and I mean anything, don't hesitate to call me."
-"I know, Ty and I appreciate that, you always have my back. I'll talk to you later, ok?"
-"Ok, later, sweetie," Tyrone says and hangs up the phone.

The server brings out Kacie's wings, and she orders herself another round of Hennessey. A handsome man walks up to the bar and stands beside Kacie.

"That rounds on me!" The unknown man says to the bartender. "Oh, that was very nice of you, thank you," utters Kacie. "It's my pleasure, what's your name?" He asks her. "Kacie," she responds. "Nice to meet you, Ms. Kacie, I'm Jeff." "Likewise," she says as they shake hands. "I like your NY accent," says Jeff. "Kacie giggles and says, "I see that you have a good ear, must mean you're a good listener." "Ha ha, well I do hear that a lot so I take it that most other dudes aren't?" "Well, my man isn't, he's the worse at listening," Kacie says. "Oh, you have a man, that's a shame. May I ask what brings you to the windy city?" "Well, doesn't everyone have someone? And I came here for business," she replies. "Oh, okay, shit maybe there's something wrong with me, 'cause I'm as single as it comes," says Jeff. "Bologna!" She yells. "Excuse me?" He asks. "I don't believe for a second that you are single. You dress nice, drive a nice car; yeah I saw you pull up. You're easy on the eyes and you're a smooth talker." "And let's not leave out a good listener," he chimes in and says. "Ha! Yes exactly, that too. All of those qualities and you want me to believe that no one has scooped you up yet?" She asks with a raised eyebrow. Jeff requests from the bartender another round before answering Kacie.

"Listen, babygirl I like what I like, and right now you are definitely it." "Oh right now I'm it, but what about 6 months from now, what about if I give up the goods, will I still be it after?" Kacie asks. "Well I'm no psychic, but you have me very intrigued. You got me ready to call your man and tell him he should have never let you come down here alone."

"Who said I was alone?" "Your smile does, your body language, everything," Jeff answers. "Okay Mr. Romancer, well you have officially gotten me drunk. And I need to get myself back to my hotel." "I'm not wasted, I can take you if you don't have a ride," says Jeff. "Aww, thanks let me just pay for these wings and my drink, and grab my jacket," says Kacie. "It's already covered, Mami c'mon now you know I'm a gentleman," Jeff says. "That you are," she says and gives him a wink. The two hop in his red Jaguar and head towards Kacie's hotel, which is about fifteen minutes away.

As they ride in Jeff's smooth automobile Kacie gets a call from her boyfriend, Dante', but she declines the call. A minute later she receives a text from him.

Dante'- "What's poppin', shawty? You don't know how to answer your phone?"
Kacie- "I'm talkin' to my mother, boo I'll hit you when I get off with her."
Dante'- "Cool."

   "Your man checking up on you, huh?" Jeff asks. "Yeah, something like that," replies Kacie.
"So how long are you in town for?" "For another two days, I'm actually gonna go see some family in Wisconsin." "Is that what you told your boyfriend? Lol" "Lol, no, I'm seriously going to see my fam, you are a trip, you know that?" "I try. Hey, so is there any way I can get your number? Maybe we can go out for dinner before you bounce?" "Umm, I'd like that, I'll write it down for you."

A few minutes later they arrive at the hotel, Jeff gets out of the car and walks Kacie to the hotel's entrance.

"I had a good time with you today, Kacie."
"It was aight, lol, just playin' I did too, really took my mind off some things." "You should let me do that more often; a beautiful person like you shouldn't have any worries." Kacie smirks, "I'll be just fine, and thanks again, text me later." "Oh, I will, goodnight, sexy." "Goodnight, handsome," she says.

Kacie enters her room and plops on the freshly made bed. "Man, what a fuckin' day!" She says aloud. She calls Dante' and begins to tell him about her day, but not mentioning meeting a new friend. He comforts her with a few encouraging words, and shortly after they hang up. She then calls one of her cousins for directions to their place. Kacie rolls out of the bed to freshen up and change into something more comfortable. When finished she called the cab driver, Alexis.

"Hey, Alexis it's Kacie, are you free?"
"I will be in ten minutes," she replies.
"Great! I have some money for you to make, I need to go to Wisconsin, you up for the drive?"
"Sure, not a problem, are you at your hotel?"
"Yup, I'm here." "Okay, I'll call you when I reach," says Alexis, and they both hang up the phone.

Fifteen minutes later Kacie receives a call from Alexis telling her to come downstairs. Kacie reaches the cab and instantly lights up with joy as Alexis holds up a bottle of Chardonnay.

"I figured you needed a little something for the ride," Alexis says. "Shit, I'm starting to think you can read minds, lol, this is exactly what I needed, girl thank you," says Kacie. "No prob, Hun now let's get on outta here before traffic hits," replies Alexis.

CHAPTER 2

FAMILY TIME!

Alexis pulls into Kacie's family's driveway and honks the horn as requested.

"Wowwww! My fam is doing real good, this house is gorgeous!" Kacie says aloud. "Yes, it is absolutely stunning," says Alexis.

"Is that my baby cuzzzz!" One of Kacie's cousins yells out from the doorway. "Yessss, Moo-Moo it's meeee! I've missed you guys so much!" Kacie shouts as she runs towards the garage to embrace her family. "We miss you too, pumpkin what's it been, three years? Ah, man we can't go this long anymore," Mochelle aka Moo-Moo says as she hugs Kacie tightly.

Kacie was greeted by three of her cousins in total; Trisha, Tracy and Mochelle, and their parents, Lonnie and Thomas. "C'mon now, y'all move and stop hogging my niecey poo," says Aunt Lonnie joyfully. "Lol, I love when you call me that, auntie. Hi, Uncle Tommy, you look great!" Kacie says. "Thanks, baby I lost 50 pounds since you last saw me," he says. She gives him a high five. "I'm very proud of you, Unc." "Come on in, baby we've got some good cooked food inside waiting for you," says Lonnie. "And some drinks, boo! We gon be lit tonight!" Shouts her cousin, Trisha! "Lol, now that's what I'm talking 'bout! Says Kacie enthusiastically.

Kacie enters the beautiful ranch style home and is suddenly hit in the nose by the aroma of all the scrumptious food.

"Yum, you guys really made a feast," says Kacie. "You know your auntie loves to cook and bake, and I did this all for you," says Lonnie. "Awww, auntie I just love, love you!" Says Kacie as she hugs her firmly. "Sit down, child I'll make your plate," Lonnie says to Kacie. "I'm kind of picky, auntie I'll make it." "Are you sure?" Lonnie asks. "Yes, but thank you," Kacie says.

Kacie makes herself a hefty plate; sampling almost everything on the table: fried chicken, BBQ pulled pork, mac and cheese, creamed spinach, vegetable rice, potato salad, fried shrimp and more.

"Mmm! Now that was good," Kacie says. "I'm glad you enjoyed it, my dear," says Lonnie. "So, guys what's first on our list of fun for tomorrow?" Kacie asks everyone in the kitchen. "Well, boo first we need a Mani and Pedi," says Trisha. "No, I thought we agreed to hit the mall first," Moo-Moo replied. "Girl, my nails are hit, so I changed the plan, we're doing the nail salon first," says Trisha. "See, there you go, always trynna change shit! Moo-Moo shouts. "Guys, guys it's not that serious, how 'bout we let Kacie decide, I mean she is our guest," Tracy, the peacemaker proclaims. "She's right, what you wanna do, babe?" Moo-Moo asks Kacie. "Honestly, I just want to be around you guys, let's do the nail salon, get that out the way, then go spend some money at the mall," Kacie says with a delightful smile. "Okay, bet," agreed the sisters.

After dinner everyone went to the family room for drinks, and to browse through some photo albums. When they got finished reminiscing, Kacie went to sleep in the guest bedroom on a posh queen sized bed.

In the morning around 7am Kacie's aunt and uncle woke up first, and cooked breakfast for everyone. After the girls stuffed their bellies, they got dressed and headed out the door for their "Girl Time." They decided to ride in Tracy's '09 Mercedes Benz, blasting some 90's R&B on the radio as they made their way to Nail Spa Castle.

"Hi, how can we help you? A beautiful mahogany brown complexioned lady asks. Shocked to see a black owned nail salon, Kacie nudges Tracy with a surprised look on her face. "What? Never seen a black woman do nails before?" She asks her. "Hell nah, girl, but much props to her," answers Kacie. "Shoot, me neither, girl that's why we always come here, gotta support our people," says Tracy. "And that's a fact," says Trisha.

The girls sit side by side and get their feet done first. The chairs they sat in had spa features that massage your whole body, and they were also heated.

"Mmmm, now all we need is some wine," says Kacie. "Girl, you ain't seen nothing yet," says Moo-Moo. A nice looking guy comes from one of the back rooms with 3 wine glasses, and a bottle of red wine in his hands.

"Pinch me, I think I'm dreaming," says Kacie. "Lol, no, Ma'am this is real. Tell me when to stop," says the gentleman as he pours Kacie some wine. "Ok, stop," she says as the wine almost reaches the top. Her cousins laugh. "Damn, K you not playin', huh? Trisha Asks. "Ha ha, I sure wasn't," she replies. The gentleman smiles and tells the ladies to enjoy. "Oh, we will!" Moo-Moo says as she winks her eye.

   "Damn, he was fine is he always here? Kacie asks. "Yeah, most of the time, and there's another dude but he ain't as cute as him," responds Moo-Moo. "Girl, you need to put me on," says Kacie. "Put you on? Girl ain't you dating that Derek dude?" Asks Moo-Moo. "You mean Dante', and yeah, but he be out there entertaining these basic bitches, thinking he low." "Well, you put up with it," replies Moo-Moo. "The dick is good, girl and he does help with the bills, when he can," she says. "My beautiful cousin deserves the complete package: loyalty, faithfulness, honesty, respect and etc....," says Moo-Moo. "I know, Hun, I know...but off of me, how's the kids and hubby?" Kacie asks. "Everyone's doing well, the twins are in junior high school now, the lil' one is starting daycare next month, and Jason and I are doing much better than we were last year," says Moo-Moo. "Last year? What the hell happened last year?" Kacie questions with a puzzled look upon her face. "Girl, I thought I told you." "Hell no you didn't, spill it!" Kacie demands. "Yo, this man had the nerve to have an affair!" "Huh! Noooo, he was one of the good ones," says Kacie. "Yeah, so we all thought, anyway, so May of last year he started to act a lil' standoffish, I'm thinking it's 'cause he just lost his mom. But I don't put shit past anybody, so I went snooping thru that phone, and sure 'nuff a full blown text history with another chick pops up." "Bitch, no!" Shouts Kacie. "Bitch, yes! Let me finish. So you know I was snapping pics of the convo with my phone, just in case he wanna delete shit when I question him. You should have seen what the fuck they were talkin' 'bout: living together, having kids, and swapping nudes, girl the whole nine."

"Damn, Hun I'm sorry this happened to you, you and Jay been together since high school, boo," says Kacie. "Girl, I know, but sometimes men get off track, and need to be smacked back on it. When I approached him about it, he surely denied it, like all men do. I pulled out the pics I took of the convos, and he practically died, he dropped to the ground and started hugging my knees begging me not to leave. He promised that it was only a summer fling, and he had planned on ending it that week. I instructed him to call her in front of me and do just that. She picked up trynna sound all sexy and shit, the Hoe sounded like an old cat in heat. But yeah, girl shit was rough for a while, I lost all trust in him, started staying out late with my girls; making his mind wander. But you know I got too much self-respect for myself to fornicate with anyone other than my husband." "I love you, Moo you're so strong, I think I would have been locked under the cell if my husband did that shit to me," Kacie says. "I can forgive once, but trust me once is all you get," Moo-Moo says.

The ladies finish up their Mani and Pedi and hop in the car to head to the mall.

    "Biggie, gimmie one more chance, Biggie, Biggie give me one more chance!" Kacie sings. "Sing it, boo! You always loved singing, girl," says Trisha. "Yes, yes, girl you know I do," Kacie replies. "Hey, K guess what?" Trisha asks. "What, Trish?" "I got homeboy's number for you!" "Lol, when did you do that?" Kacie asks. "When you and Moo was chattin' away," says Trisha. "Ooh, you sneaky, lol." "Well, you want it or not?" Kacie snatches the paper with the guy's number on it out of Trisha's hand. "Gimmie that, girl he was extra fine," says Kacie. All the girls laugh.

A few minutes later they pulled up to the shopping center. Kacie's phone rings. "Hey, you guys go ahead, I'll meet up with you," Kacie says. "But, you'll get lost," says Tracy. "Trace, I'm good, I'm not your lil' 12 year old cousin anymore, lol," says Kacie. "Ok, fine, do you, lol." The girls walk off and Kacie answers her phone.

-"Hello?" Answers Kacie.
-"Hey there, sweet lady," a male voice says.
-"Oh, Hello, Mr. Jeff thought you forgot about me."
-"I'd be the biggest fool to do that, what you up to?"
-"Hanging out with my cousins, just got to the mall, you?"
-"I'm home, messing around on my guitar, you were on my mind heavy so I decided to call."
-"Wow, you know how to play that thing?"
-"I'm aight, still learning."
-"That's sexy, you'll have to play for me one day."
-"How about tonight? We can go to dinner at an incredible restaurant in the city called, 'Francisco's'," then I'll serenade you a bit at my place.

-"Trynna get me at your place so soon, huh? I could be a serial killer or some shit, Lol."

-"Lol, I'll take my chances, beautiful. So 9 o'clock? I can pick you up from where you are."

-"Umm, let me get back to you," says Kacie.

-"Ah, c'mon, just one night, I promise I'll be a gentleman."

Kacie pauses on the phone to think about if she really wants to meet up with him.

-"Hello?" Jeff says.

-"I'm here…umm, ok let's make it 8 though."

-"Okay, bet, I'll text you later for the address."

-"Cool," Kacie says.

-"See you later, pretty brown eyes," Jeff says.

- "Lol, later, Jeff," she says and hangs up the phone.

Kacie meets back up with her cousins.

"And who was that on the phone that you had to temporarily disown us?" Asks Moo-Moo.

"Lol, a friend," Kacie answers blushing. "What kind of friend?" Moo-Moo asks picking on Kacie. "His name's Jeff, I met him in chi-town the other night." "Look at you, pulling all the dudes." "Stop, I do not, lol. Wow! What kind of store is this? They got all the fly shit in one place," asks Kacie. "Mmhm, trynna change the subject, we'll touch back on that later though, 'fo sho," says Moo-Moo. "Ha ha okay, girl," Kacie says.

Kacie saw so many nice things that she wanted to buy; ignoring the fact that she just lost her job she buys $2,000 worth of stuff.

"Damn, K you sure as hell went shopping today," Tracy says to Kacie as they make their way back to the house. "It was just so much nice stuff, I couldn't choose," Kacie says. "I feel you, girl so what you wanna do tonight? Tracy asks. "Well actually I'm gonna meet up with a friend later on." "Oh, okay I didn't know you had friends out here," says Tracy. "Same shit I said, sis she done met ole boy the other night and won't spill the tea," interrupts Moo-Moo. "Fine, nosey asses, like I said earlier his name is Jeff. He is easy on the eyes, not too pretty, not too rough, shaved head, caramel complexion, with a salt and pepper gold tee. I guess early to mid-forties, I didn't get a chance to ask his age." "Well doesn't he sound like a tall glass of 'Fine as shit,' Lol," Trisha says. "Yeah, he's a charmer, another reason why I find it hard to believe he's single," says Kacie. "What's the other reason?" Moo-Moo asks. "Nowadays nobody is single, even my mom agrees." "Yeah, and you are one of those people who aren't single, you playing with fire going out with another man, Kacie," says Moo-Moo. "Cuz, stop, Dante' is not gonna find out, and I know his ass is out there in a bitch's face as we speak." "Hmm, I suppose," responds Moo-Moo with a displeased look on her face.

After filling her cousins in on Jeff, Kacie searches through her suitcase for something appropriate to wear on her date.

"Damn, what am I going to wear, guys? I didn't pack anything suitable to go on a date," Kacie says whining. "Come see what's in my closest; we're about the same size," Trisha tells Kacie.

"Ooh! Girl, where were you planning on wearing this to?" Kacie asks as she holds up a leopard print bodysuit. "Lol, oh that old thing, it was for a costume party," she replies. "Yeah, okay if you say so, lol...ooh, I think I found the perfect dress," Kacie pulls out a short black suede dress from Trisha's closet. "Ahh, nice choice, Cuz you can keep it when you're done with it," says Trisha. "Aww, really?" She asks. "Yeah, I have the same one in red and I have too many black clothes anyway." "Okay, thanks, girl," says Kacie. Kacie tries on the dress and it fits her like a glove.

"Babe, you have pumps to go with the dress? Or you need to borrow some as well?" Trisha asks. "Yeah, I packed enough cute shoes, who wants to do my makeup?" Kacie asks. "Ooh, boo let me hook you up!" Shouts Tracy. "And I'll do your hair," says Moo-Moo. "I was just gonna flat iron it," says Kacie. "I'll do it, K trust me I'll hook it up for real, for real," Moo-moo says. "Okay, Moo." As Kacie is getting all dolled up, Jeff shoots her a text.

Jeff- "Hey, beauty queen, are you almost ready?"
Kacie- "Hi, Jeff, yup in another hour or so."
Jeff- "Perfect, I'll start making my way, what's the address?"
Kacie-"225 Blooming Street, Milwaukee, W.I 53215"
Jeff- "Ok, I'll see you soon, sweetie."
Kacie- "Looking forward to it."

Kacie's cousins finish making her look gorgeous, and Trisha's short black dress hugs Kacie's ass and hips.

"Okay, now! Where you going out to, baby?" Aunt Lonnie asks Kacie. "Oh, hey, Auntie a friend of mine from Chicago is taking me out for dinner," she responds. "That sounds nice, you kids enjoy," says Aunt Lonnie. "Thanks, auntie!" Shouts Kacie.

Kacie's phone rings and startles her aunt Lonnie.

"Ooh! All that loud music," she says. "Sorry, Auntie, it's just my ringtone...Hey," Kacie says, answering the phone. "Meet me outside," says Jeff. "I'm coming," she says and hangs up the phone. "Bye, guys I love you, I'll be back in a few hours!" Shouts Kacie. "We love you too!" Everyone screams out.

Jeff is outside waiting for his lovely date in his new, all black Mercedes Benz. Kacie is flattered that he pulled out such a nice toy to take her on a date.

"Damn, Jeff! That's how you rollin'?" Asks Kacie as she walks to his car. "Nah, Love that's how we rollin', and damn you look stunning!" He says. Jeff and Kacie hug one another and he opens the door to the passenger side, and then gets in the driver's seat and pulls off. "Thanks, handsome I wanted to impress you," Kacie says. "Lol, oh stop it, you know you fine, girl," Jeff says. Kacie smirks and winks at Jeff. "I be knowin', lol," she replies. "We'll be at the restaurant shortly, I made a reservation for us at a dope spot not too far from here," Jeff tells Kacie.
"Sounds great, I can't wait to eat, lol," says Kacie.

"Yes, me too, so how has your stay been so far?" Jeff asks. "Pretty good, I'm enjoying my time with the fam, and meeting you has been a breath of fresh air," she replies. Jeff smiles widely. "Is that right? And why is that?" He asks. "Well, you're something different; new, I needed that," she says. "A change is always good, I do hope that we'll be seeing each other again after tonight," Jeff says. "Maybe, but I can't tell the future," Kacie says. "Hey, people make time for who they want, and my time will always be available for you," says Jeff.

CHAPTER 3

THE DATE

"Good evening, welcome to 'Francisco's'," the greeter at the front desk says to the couple. "Hi, good evening, reservation for Jeff Michaels," says Jeff. The greeter scans her list. "Yes, you're a little early, but the table is ready so you guys can follow me," says the greeter lady. "Perfect seats for a perfect woman," Jeff says to Kacie. "And how do you know I'm perfect? You hardly know me," she says. "I know enough, and I'm trying to get to know you better than you know yourself," he says. "Damn, really? Lol, well when you find out, please let me know, because my ass is lost," Kacie says. "No, you're not, you're a very strong, smart, confident woman, you're just going thru some things," Jeff says. "I guess you're right," she says.

A seemingly young waitress comes over to their table.

"Good evening, my name is Jesse, and I will be your server for the night. I see you have a prefixed menu, your appetizers will be out shortly," Jesse says. "Thank you, Jesse," says Jeff with a charming smile. "A prefixed menu, huh? Look at you!" Kacie says joking with Jeff. "Yup, and you better like my selections, lady, lol" he says. "As you can see, I like to eat, so bring it," Kacie replies. "Mmm, you know I see, thick all over, just how I like em'," he says. "Lol, don't eat me now, those eyes of yours look like they're stripping me naked, and buttering me up like a dinner roll," she says. "Ha ha, I would love to taste you, Kacie," Jeff says.

"Damn, just like that, huh? You ain't got no type of filter," she says.

"Lol, I'm a grown man, filters are for kids, and how you know I'm not talking 'bout those sexy lips of yours?" Jeff asks.

"Ring! Ring! Ring!"

Kacie's phone goes off before she could answer.

"Sorry, let me take this," Kacie says.

"Sure," replies Jeff. Kacie walks to the restroom.

-"Hey, baby wassup? I miss you!" Kacie says.

-"Shit, baby I miss you more, can't wait to see you tomorrow," says Dante'.

-"Uh huh, you just miss this kitty kat, lol," Kacie says.

-"Lol, just a little, Mami, 8 am right?"

-"Yes, Hun, please be on time, for once."

-"Lol, I will, girl don't worry, just bring that ass home to daddy."

-"Lol, okay, baby I'll see you then."

-"Where are you rushing off to?"

-"I'm eating dinner with the fam."

-"Let me say wassup to everyone."

-"Boy, they don't want to speak to you, you know they barley like you, lol."

-"Yeah, whatever."

-"Aww, don't sound like that, I love you, babe, talk later."

-"Love you too, lata," Dante' says and hangs up the phone.

Kacie returns back to the table.

"Sorry about that," Kacie tells Jeff.

"It's cool, pretty lady." "Ah, I see the second round is here, it looks amazing," she says. "Yes, it's linguine with smoked salmon in a cream sauce," Jeff says. "Wow, nice touch," Kacie responds.

"Thanks, so, Ms. Kacie tell me more about yourself, there's a mystery about you that's driving me crazy."

"Lol, oh there is, huh? Well, I don't have any kids yet, but I want a few someday. You know I'm in a relationship, um, my favorite color is light pink, and I lost my virginity at 21," Kacie says with a smile.

Jeff smiles back and says, "Oh, 21? Nice, you were waiting for the right guy?" "I was actually, he winded up never coming around, but at the time I thought he was the right one," she says. "Okay, okay, well I was 12," he says. "Damn, that's young," Kacie says.

"Nah, that's average for a guy." "Maybe 15, but 12 is a damn baby!" "Hey, I ain't complaining, I had a lot of fun in my day," Jeff says. "I see, and did you get any girls pregnant back then?" Kacie asks. "Uh, one, she was 17, I was 15," Jeff answers. "Damn, you were a young daddy," she says. "Yup, we had a daughter, and two years after that we had a son," Jeff says. "Wow, so what happened to you guys?" Kacie asks. "She was killed in a fire when the kids were 2 and 4," says Jeff. "O.m.g, I'm sorry to hear that, those poor kids," Kacie says.

"Yeah, it was very tough, had to raise them babies on my own, had some help from my mother and a few ladies here and there," he says.

"How are the kids doing now?" She asks.

"They're good, grown and busy. My son is working in real estate, and my daughter is a kindergarten teacher. I also have three younger kids ages 12, 9 and 4," Jeff says. "Oh wow, you have a football team almost," Kacie says jokingly. "Lol, yup and I've been married once, I'm actually going thru a divorce right now with my youngest son's mother," says Jeff.

"Oh, I thought you said you weren't married?" She questions. "Well, we're separated," Jeff says.

"Still married, Jeff," Kacie says.

"I'm working on it, as we speak, trust me, her and I both want this to be over," he says.

"That bad, huh?" She asks.

"Yeah, that bad, fighting, and cheating on both parts," says Jeff.

"Hi, guys, how is everything so far?" Jesse asks.

"Everything is perfect, thank you," replies Jeff.

A bus boy brings over their third course.

"Excuse me? This isn't what I ordered," Jeff says to the bus boy. "Uh, Sir, that is what you had circled for the third course," he replies.

"No, there must be a misunderstanding, I ordered skirt steak with mashed potatoes and asparagus," Jeff says in a firm tone.

"I have here: baked chicken with mash and broccoli, Sir," the bus boy says. Jeff bangs on the table and gets the attention of their waiter. "Jesse! Let me speak to the manager, because this imbecile clearly cannot read!" Jeff shouts. "Jeff, please, it's fine I like baked chicken," Kacie pleads. "I didn't bring you here for no fucking chicken! I could have made that shit myself," yells Jeff. "Sorry, Sir I will get the manager right away," says Jesse.

The manager walks over to their table.

"Hello, my name is Louis; I am the manager here, what seems to be the problem?" He asks.
"The problem is that this dry ass chicken…is not what I ordered," Jeff says.
"I am very sorry for the inconvenience, what is it that you ordered?" Louis asks.
"Skirt steak, mashed potatoes and asparagus, is that so hard?" Jeff asks.
"No, it's not, how do you like your steak?" Louis asks.
"Well-done, no pink whatsoever," Jeff replies.
"Coming right up!" Says Louis.
Louis rushes the waiter and bus boy from the table.

"Yo, you didn't have to go that hard, I told you I'd eat the chicken, Jeff," says Kacie.
"What you mean? I chose steak and that's what I expect to see on our table," he replies.
"You're right, but you just went too far calling that man an idiot and what not," Kacie says.

"Well, he was, the customer is always right, he needs to be retrained," Jeff says.

"I hope they send out the right stuff this time, don't wanna see that side of you again," says Kacie.

"I hope so too, baby sorry if I frightened you," he says.

"Yeah, you did a little. Can you pour me a glass of that wine." she says. "Sure, tell me when to stop," Jeff says. "Just fill it to the rim," she says.

"Mmm, you trynna get nice, huh?" Jeff asks.

"Sure am, it's back home to my crazy man tomorrow, I need this drink, lol," Kacie says.

"Lol, that's your choice, woman," Jeff says.

"Oh, please, like you're a better choice?" Kacie says. Before Jeff could answer the manager brings their food to the table.

"Okay, here we are, skirt steak, mashed potatoes and asparagus, and I bought you a complimentary bottle of wine for the mix up," says Louis.

"Ahh, very nice," says Jeff.

Jeff cuts into his steak and a little blood oozes out. "What the fuck did I say?! What is this?!" Jeff shouts at the manager. "Iye, oh boy, I am so sorry about this, let me bring you out another," Louis says.

"And wait another 15 minutes? You out yo' mother fuckin' mind!" Jeff shouts

"Jeff, Jeff please chill," Kacie says begging him.

Jeff flings his plate across the room, hitting another guest's table, the man at the table stands up and tells Jeff to cool it. Jeff walks over to the man and punches him in the face.

"Oh my, God! Jeff, what the fuck?!" Kacie yells.
"Yo, let's go!" He yells to Kacie.

The two run out of the restaurant.

"Yo! I'm so fucking pissed! Fucked up my whole fuckin' night" Jeff shouts.
"Dude, you did too fuckin' much just now, over a fuckin' steak, Jeff really?" Kacie asks.
"Not right now, Kacie, I need to cool off," he says.
"Clearly, I'll find my own way back," she says.
"What? Stop playing and get in the car!" Jeff demands. "Not getting in the car with a mad man!" Shouts Kacie. Kacie starts walking toward the street, Jeff follows her. "Hey, baby I'm sorry, please get in the car," he pleads. "No, Jeff leave me alone," she says. "C'mon, please! I'll do whatever you want, just get in," he says. "Oh, God fine, Jeff, but just take me straight to the house, and don't talk to me," she says getting into the car. "Thank you," says Jeff. "Mmmhmm," she says turning on the radio.

They drive off heading to Kacie's family's house.

"So, can we talk about us?" Jeff asks.
There's no answer from Kacie.
"Hello!" Jeff says.
"Hello! I told you not to talk to me."

"C'mon, Kacie I'm serious," he says.

"Nigga, you think I'ma fuck with you after that stunt you pulled? You ain't got no home training," she says.

"Damn, I know I showed my ass, but let me make it up to you?" He asks. "How you gon' do that, Jeff? I leave in the morning," she says.

"Okay, so come back to my place, I wanna taste you 'til the morning comes," Jeff says.

"Lol, Jeff please, this ain't the time for that freak talk," Kacie says. Jeff slides his right hand up Kacie's dress and whispers, "Girl, I'm fucking serious," in her ear. Kacie bites her bottom lip in excitement.

"Mmm, don't do that," she says.

"Babe, let me take care of you," Jeff tells Kacie. Kacie agrees to accompany Jeff to his place for a nightcap.

Shit, what am I getting myself into with this damn lunatic?

Kacie and Jeff arrive at his place.

"Help me with these heels, please?" She asks Jeff.

"Nah, leave them on," he says, and throws her on the bed. Kacie giggles and squirms. Jeff turns her over and starts to unzip her black dress.

"Lol, you waste no time, huh?" Kacie asks.

"Nope, I don't, girl," he says while massaging her big ass.

"Damn, that feels good," she says while letting out a moan.

"Mmm, this ass is soft, and so fat!" He says smacking it. Jeff turns her on her back and spreads her legs as wide as they could go and begins to lick her clit.
"Shit! Kacie yells out.
"Mmmmmm, tastes like cherries," Jeff says.

Man, he eating this pussy like a freshly baked cherry pie! Lol.

"That's it, baby cum all in my mouth!" Jeff says.
"Oooh! Jeff," Kacie lets out as she commences to cum while pushing down Jeff's head. His mouth filled with her sweet cream.

"I knew you'd taste like pie, now gimmie that pussy, girl," Jeff says.
"Nope, it's my turn now," she says as she drops herself from the bed to the floor.
"Oh, I really, really like you," Jeff says as he lies back on the bed.

Kacie kisses the head of his dick, then takes the whole 9 inches into her mouth without gagging.

"Ooh! Fuck! Damn, girl," Jeff says.
"Yeah, you like that?" She asks.
"I love it, please don't stop," he responds.

Kacie sucks his thick penis slow and fast, doing multiple tricks with her tongue.

"Damn, you suck this dick so, so gooood," Jeff says.

"It's just so perfect," Kacie tells him.
"Glad you like it, mami it can be all yours, if you want it to be," he says.

Kacie doesn't say a word she just continues to pleasure him. A few moments later Jeff stops Kacie. He slides on a magnum and pulls Kacie up from the floor and sits her on his hard dick. She lets out a gasp, as she eases his manhood into her wet, warm pussy. She rides him up and down like a merry-go-round.

"Mmmm! Ride this dick, baby," he says, while holding on to her ample butt. They switch positions to doggy style, and he jams his dick inside of her.

"Shiiit!" She yells.
"Mmmhmm! You better take this dick, girl."
"Oh, I will!" She responds back.
Kacie throws her ass back and Jeff fucks her harder, and harder. He slaps her ass 'til it blushes. They cum simultaneously, while both moaning profusely.

Kacie collapses on the bed and just lays there for a few minutes. Jeff leaves the room for a moment and returns with a warm wash rag. Kacie is already asleep, so he wipes her private area off for her.

CHAPTER 4

HOME "SWEET" HOME...

"Kacie, Kacie!" Yells her cousin Moo-Moo.
"Huh?" She asks raising her head from the pillow.
"Wake up, girl you don't wanna miss your flight," says Moo-Moo.
"Oh shit, girl I don't even know how I got here," says Kacie.
"Your friend Jeff brought you here, your ass was passed out."
"Damn, I must have had a wild night."
"Yeah, clearly, now get up, boo," Moo-Moo says.

Kacie hopped in the shower, got dressed and said her goodbyes to her family.

"Kacie, Wait! You're forgetting your phone," Tracy says. "Oh, shoot! Thanks girl, what would I do without my phone! Lol, love you! Byeeee!" Kacie says.

"Good morning, Ms. Fuller," says the cab driver.
"Good morning," Kacie responds with a smile while climbing in the backseat.
"We will be at the airport in no time," says Tammie the cab driver. "Great, thank you," says Kacie.

Kacie arrives to the airport with no time to kill.

Wooo, just made it! Why is my ass always late?

Kacie takes her seat on the plane and tries to send Dante' a text but it wouldn't go through.
Damn, well he knows what time to be here.

She puts her earplugs in her ears and closes her eyes. An hour and a half later they arrive in New York City.

"Ladies and gentlemen, we have arrived in New York City, the time is now 7:50 AM, I hope you all enjoy the rest of your day," the pilot announces on the overhead speaker.

Mmm, that lil' nap was everything.

Kacie grabs her belongings and waits for her turn to exit the plane.

It's good to be home, now I gotta really see what the fuck I'ma do about this no job situation, argh.

Kacie heads outside planning to see Dante', but he is nowhere to be found.

Damn, is this nigga really late picking me up, gotta be fuckin' kidding me.

Kacie dials his number, but he doesn't answer so she leaves a message:

"Dante', oooh honneyyyy! Where the fuck are you?! My plane landed ten minutes ago. You need to hurry up and get over here! And why you ain't answering this phone!"

Kacie calls Dante' two more times and he finally answers.

Dante'-"Hello," he says with a soft voice.
Kacie-"Hello, my ass, where are you!" She yells.
Dante'-"Shit, babe you here already?! Dante' asks in
a panic.
Kacie-"Wow, Dante' really? This is a fuckin' shame!"
Dante'-"I'm so sorry, baby I got in real late last night,
but I'm coming right now,"
Kacie-"Nah, you good stay right where you at."
Dante'-"Yo, chill I'm coming, you should have fuckin'
reminded me this morning."
Kacie-"I shouldn't have to remind you about
something so important, and I texted you when I got
on the plane!"
Dante'-"Well, I didn't get no text from you, I'm on my
way right now, girl."
Kacie-"No! I said it's fine, I'll find another way home,"
she says and hangs up the phone.

Kacie now calls Tyrone, her cab driver/friend. Dante'
calls her back while she was on the phone with him,
but she declines the call.

Ty-"Good morning, beautiful," says Tyrone.
Kacie-"Hi, Ty, how are you?
Ty-"Better now, are you back in NY yet?"
Kacie-"Yes, actually that's why I'm calling, can you
believe that so called man of mine overslept and got
me out here looking foolish."
Ty-"Oh my, I'm sorry to hear that, damn he's slipping
for that, well, I can be there to get you in 10 minutes.
Kacie-"Oh, yes that would be perfect! I know I can
always count on you, Ty.
Ty-"Always, sweetie, what terminal are you?

Kacie-"Terminal 4."
Ty-"Sure, see you soon."

Kacie and Tyrone get off the phone and Kacie goes back inside the airport to take a seat.

Kacie arrives home just 5 minutes after Tyrone picked her up at the airport. When she enters her apartment she finds Dante' in the kitchen fixing breakfast.

"What the fuck you doing here, Dante'?" She asks.
"Just a way of saying I'm so sorry that I wasn't there at the airport," he replies.
"Where's your car? I didn't see it parked outside."
"My brother dropped me off; he needed to borrow it for a little run." "Oh, okay, well the food looks and smells good but I'm still mad at you."
"And you should be, but I'ma make it up, K I promise," says Dante'. "Yeah, yeah whatever, Dante' you say that time after time," Kacie says.
"Here's some money for the cab, baby."
"I don't want your filthy money, boy!" Kacie says with such pizzazz. "So what you want, girl?" Dante' says while rubbing his penis on Kacie's ass.
"Nigga, move! Don't touch me with that thing," Kacie shouts. "Damn, it's like that, K? You trippin', it was an honest mistake now you gon' punish a nigga?!"
"I sure the fuck am, I was in a bad mood before but now I'm in a dangerous mood," says Kacie.
"Damn, babe I didn't mean to 'cause all that."

"Nigga, you ain't 'cause all of nothing, I lost my fuckin' job the other day, I told you that!" Shouts Kacie. "Yeah, babe that's crazy...shit I really gotta step it up now," Dante' says. "Yes you really do, I have a little saved up but you know how fast money goes," retorts Kacie. "On God, I'ma make shit happen for us, you can hold me to that," Says Dante' with such passion.

CHAPTER 5

BABY MOMMA DRAMA

Jeff- "Hey, baby what you doing?"
Kacie-"Hey, Jeff what did I tell you about calling me baby?"
Jeff-"You know I don't wanna hear all that, you my baby, boo, lover and friend."
Kacie-"Yeah, okay, we barley know one another."
Jeff-"And whose fault is that, boo?"
Kacie-"Lol, umm, my boyfriend's."
Jeff-"Lol, and that's why you have a man now. We too grown to have girlfriends and boyfriends."
Kacie-"Long distance relationships ain't really my thang."
Jeff- "We should try it out for a bit, and then eventually one of us can move to where the other person lives."
Kacie-"Wow, you got it all planned out, huh? Lol.
Jeff-"I mean it's not often that a woman of your caliber walks on by. So, yes I have been making plans for us."

Kacie hears Dante' walk in the house.

"I'll call you back, I'll call you back," Kacie says in a swift whisper.

"Yo, K where you at?!" Dante' yells from the front door. "In here!" Kacie yells out from the bedroom.

Dante' finds Kacie and plants a big kiss on her lips.

"Wow, you're in a good mood, wassup?" She asks. "I came across a way to make some extra cash," he says.

"Oh, boy what is the crazy scam this time, Dante'?" Kacie asks. "Alright, boom, so I got this ill ass hook up with gift cards, it's a sure come up," Dante' responds. "Okay, so what's the catch?" Kacie asks.

"Ain't really no catch, just might be a little risky. Umm, I do need like $1,000 to take them off my man's hands, then I can make money off the flip," Dante' says. "No catch, huh? Where's all your money at, nigga?" Kacie asks.

"Chill, chill you know my money fluctuates, and I need to hop on this shit right now!"

Kacie rolls her eyes.

"Okay, and you know I just lost my job," she says.
"Yeah, and I also know you got money in the bank, with your stingy ass," he says.
"Fuck you, it's called a savings, jerk."
"Yeah, well are you gonna loan it to me or not?"
"What's in it for me?" She asks.
"Girl, you know everything I do is for us, plus I'ma hit you off with a couple extra hundreds," he says.
"Alright, D don't fuck this up, I can't afford to take another loss," says Kacie.
"I got you, Mami, I promise!" Dante' says and kisses her forehead.

Dante' and Kacie make their way to his car to head for the bank in Green Acres Mall. Dante's phone rings multiple times but he doesn't answer.

"Damn, who you ducking?" Kacie asks.
"Lol, eh, just some nigga I don't wanna talk to," he says. "Oh, okay…pull over at chase, and I'll be right back," says Kacie.

As Kacie goes into the bank Dante' calls back the person who's been calling his phone.

"Damn, Candice I told you stop blowing up my phone when I'm with my girl," Dante' says.
"I didn't know you were with her, nigga, my bad," she says. "If I ain't answer the first time then you should get the point, aight?" He replies.
"Fine, but wassup babe? You know I'm missing that dick, mmm," says Candice.
"Lol, shit you know I'm missing that good ass pussy too, I'ma see you later, fa sho'," says Dante'.
"Okay, baby see you later, kisses," she says.
He makes a kissy noise back and hangs up the phone.

Shortly after the call ended Kacie makes her way back to the car.

"Everything good?" He asks.
Kacie says yes, and hands over an envelope with 10 fresh 100s. "Aight, cool thanks, boo where you want me to drop you?" Dante' asks. "Actually I'm good right here," she says. "Oh, you 'bout to go shoppin'? Pick me up something. "Yeah, D we'll see," she says.

"Okay, love you," Dante' says and kisses her on the cheek. "Love you, too," Kacie says as she waves goodbye.

Kacie dials her best friend Chelsea's number to see if she can meet her for lunch.

Kacie-"Hey, Chels! What you doing?"
Chelsea- "Nothing, girl at the crib with 'yo bad ass god son."
Kacie-"Treyvon is not bad, girl, stop it."
"Chelsea- "Yeah, okay you take him for an entire day and let's see if your story changes, lol. But wassup boo?"
Kacie-"Ha ha, that's a bet, girl, listen come to the mall, I wanna do some shoppin' and hit Applebee's."
Chelsea- "Shit, a bitch broke, you got me?"
Kacie-"Okay, I got u and Trey on an outfit and some food."
Chelsea- "Ahh, Snap! Gucci here I come!"
Kacie-"Lol, don't push it, girl more like Old Navy! Lol"
Chelsea- "Damn, what about something from Macy's?"
Kacie-"We can do that, that's more up my speed, plus I love their sales rack."
Chelsea-"Okay, boo, Trey and I will be there in 15 minutes!"
Kacie-"Okay, see y'all soon," she says and hangs up the phone.

Chelsea and her son, Trey, 8 pull into the huge parking lot at the mall. Kacie meets them at the front entrance.

"Hi, handsome!" Kacie yells while reaching for Trey. "Hi, god mommy," he says with a soft voice. "What's wrong, sugar?" She asks him. "Ain't nothing wrong with that boy he just didn't wanna stop playing them damn video games, but wassup, girl you lookin' good," says Chelsea. "Thanks, girl I lost a few pounds; been a little stressed," Kacie says. "Oh, boy what the hell is up now?" Chelsea asks. "I'll tell you over drinks and food later, let's hit up Macy's first," she says. "Okay, sweetie," says Chelsea as the three ride up the escalator.

"Aye, ain't that Dante's baby mother over there?" Chelsea asks while nudging Kacie in the arm. "Oh, It sure is, damn she done let herself go," Kacie says. "Lol, nah she always looked trash," says Chelsea. "Lol, you stupid, girl," Kacie says.

Patricia, Dante's baby mother spots Kacie and Chelsea, and whispers something to the woman walking with her. The two begin to stare at Kacie and giggle.

"Something funny, Pat?" Kacie asks as they walk near one another. "Oh, hi, Kacie didn't even see you over there," she says. "Yeah, okay Hoe, and you better quit calling Dante' so late at night," Kacie says. "Lol, bitch that's the father of my kid, i'll call any got damn time I want," Pat responds. "Know your fuckin' role!" Kacie yells as she steps into Patricia's face. "Chill, K! The sloppy bitch ain't worth it," Chelsea says.

"Sloppy?! Bitch, I'll show you sloppy!" Patricia shouts to Chelsea. Before Chelsea could respond security rushed over to defuse the situation.

"What seems to be the problem, ladies?" A tall, black security guard asks. "No problem here, Sir we were just leaving," Chelsea says as she grabs up Trey. Kacie, Chelsea and Trey begin to walk away before the security guard could ask any more questions. "Next time take it outside!" The security officer yells.

"Girl, what the hell was all of that?" Chels asks Kacie. "Damn, I really need a few drinks; everything is just erkin' me!" She says. "Yeah, babe you need to relax some, how are you and D doing anyway?" She asks. "Still having trust issues after the last bitch I caught him entertaining, but I'm trying to put it in the past," Kacie says. "I know it's tough, girl once the trust is gone the love is usually next to follow," Chels says. "Damn, ain't that the truth, and this stupid bitch Pat is starting to get on my nerves too. I think she blows his phone up at 3 am, just to tick me off. Every time he spends the night his phone is ringing off the hook, and 95 percent of the time it's her ass." "Well, you need to check him too, 'cause when you ain't around you know he picking up every time, don't debate me," says Chelsea. "You're probably right, boo I just hope he ain't fuckin' her," says Kacie. "Hmph, me too, ugh! I hate men, I'ma date me a white man for now on," says Chelsea. "Lol, girl, same shit I told Tonya the other day over the phone," says Kacie.

"I haven't spoken to her in a while, how is she doing?" Asks Chels. "She's okay, just juggling work, school and the twins, doing what she gotta do as a single mom. We all need to go out soon, invite some of the other girls and turn up!" Kacie says. "Yes, girl I need that, just let me know when so I can ship Trey off to Big Trey." "Lol, y'all ready to go eat something now?" Kacie asks. Chelsea and Trey both say yes, and the three make their way to Applebee's.

CHAPTER 6

CHELSEA

"Trey! Treeeeyyy!" Chelsea yells down the hallway. "What, Ma?!" Shouts Trey.
"What me again, I'ma fuck you up!"
Trey runs to the kitchen where his mother is, "Yes, Mommy?" "Where is your report card?" Chelsea asks. "Um, Mrs. Cherokee said we get them next week." "That's funny because Mrs. Cherokee called me this morning to discuss how poorly you did this semester, she said to make sure that you show me your report card. So let me ask you again, where is your report card, Trey?" With a fearful look on his tiny face, Trey stuttered, "It's, it's in my book bag, mommy." "Go get it now! What I tell you about lying to me!" She yells.

Trey hurried to his room to get his book bag. Chelsea snatched his book bag from him and rambled in the junkie bag for the report card.

"Nacho cheese stains, really, Trey? Take better care of your stuff, man, maybe if you had some As on there you would!" "I'm sorry, Ma," Trey says. "Sorry nothing," she says as she scans his report card. "D in science, C in English, D in math, B in gym; figures, and a C minus in social studies, come on, Trey, what is going on? She asks. "Well, mom I've been having trouble with homework, and you and dad are never around to help." "Baby, I do apologize for that, you're so smart, you never showed signs that you were struggling. Have you called your dad to come help you?"

"Yes, a few times, but he always says he can't because he's too busy," he says as he hangs his head. Chelsea lifts his chin up with her hand and kisses him on the cheek. "Hey, I promise to be here more and help you with whatever you need, but Mrs. Cherokee also said you have been talking back to her a lot, you know your father and I taught you to respect your elders." "Yes, Ma'am you have, I am sometimes in a cranky mood and I don't know why."
"Okay, well I'm going to be checking up on you more often now, I need my big man to become someone great when he gets older, agree?" She asks him.
"Agree!" Trey responds with a big smile on his face.
"Good, now get dressed we're going to pay your dad a visit." "Yes!" He says with excitement and runs along.

While Trey is getting dressed to go see his father, Chelsea packs some sandwiches and snacks for the ride.

"Ring! Ring! Ring!" Chelsea's phone goes off.

"Hello?" Answers Chelsea.
"Heyyyyyyy, Boo! What you doing?" Asks Kacie
"About to take your bad ass god son to see his no good father," she replies. "Okay, first of all my baby is not bad, he's just busy, and secondly that man wasn't no good when he was putting my baby Trey up in you," Kacie says with a loud giggle.

"Lol, girl you is a trip, I guess you right about that, wassup though chicka?" Chelsea asks.

"Ahh, ain't nothing, since a sister been outta work I don't know what to do with myself," Kacie says.

"Word, what's your next step, Hun?"

"I'm thinking of a few side hustles that can potentially turn into a main source of income, I got on my thinking cap, boo," Kacie answers.

"I see, I see, I hope you come up with something fast, I know that nigga of yours don't be much help," Chelsea says. "You know what, yeah, normally he ain't shit, but homeboy been coming thru with some money and groceries lately," Kacie says.

"Okay, okay now that's what I'm talking about, where he getting this money from tho?"

"Girl, bye you know I ain't even gon' ask, I'm just grateful I don't have to deplete my savings, feel me?"

"I feel you, girl, but shit that was a lot of money you turned down, you know my ghetto ass would have took that and ran." "Ha! Girl, you know I know you, but I ain't trippin', that company just felt all wrong," Kacie says. "Yeah, I guess you can't ignore your gut feelings, but girl let me get out of here and get us on the road; you know I hate these rides to New Jersey." "It's right there, Chels." "Yeah, says the grown ass woman that doesn't drive." "Oooh! You got me, you got me, bye, girl, kiss my baby for me." "Got ya, love you!" Says Chelsea "Love you more, babe," Kacie says and hangs up the phone.

"Trey, you ready?! Shouts Chelsea.
"Yeah, here I come!" Trey yells as he skips to his mother. "You look cute, little boy what you got a girlfriend in daddy's neighborhood?"
"Lol, nah, mom I just like to look good when I go out," Trey says. "Oh really, since when? You still spill juice on all your shirts." "That was a thing of the past, I'm getting older, Ma I gotta stay fly," Trey says.
"Yeah, okay, you need to put that same energy into them damn grades. Now let's see what daddy's gonna do to help out with them grades of yours."

Chelsea and Trey get on the road headed to Elizabeth, New Jersey where her estranged husband and his girlfriend live.

"I hope his little girlfriend isn't there with her nosey ass," Chelsea says to Trey. "I think daddy said Shannon and Kendall were going to the beach today," says Trey. "Oh, isn't that nice, well, good we don't need her there to pry into the family's business anyway." "Yeah, I wish I was at the beach with Kendall though, maybe they'll get back home before we leave." "Well, I hope not, I can't stand neither one of them." "You're just mean, mama, damn."
"Watch your mouth, Trey, I will reach in that backseat and smack you." "Lol, why you gotta be so violent, mommy?" Trey asks. "I'm not playing either! Let a red light come up." Trey puts his fingers on his lips and pretends to zip them shut.

Chelsea and Trey arrive at Trey Sr.'s home in New Jersey.

"Dadddy!" Trey yells as he runs toward his father. Big Trey embraces him in his arms and kisses him on the forehead. "Where yo momma at?" He asks him. "She's still in the car putting on her make-up."

"Ay, Chelsea bring your ass out that car, ain't seen you in a minute," he says. Chelsea steps out of her car in a cute mini skirt and halter top, her mocha complexion glistened in the sun.

Chelsea walks over to Trey Sr. and palms her hand on the back of his head and kisses his lips. He steps back and smirks at her. "Is your girlfriend home?" Chelsea asks. "Nah, she gon' be out for a few hours, why wassup?" Trey Sr. asks. Chelsea pulls down the top of her skirt showing that she wasn't wearing any panties and says, "Oh, you know wassup." Big Trey yells for his son to go play at the neighbor's house until they come for him. Trey runs along, and Chelsea and big Trey make their way into the big comfy house.

CHAPTER 7

JEFF'S WOES

"Hey, Boobie what's going on?" Asks Jeff
"Boobie? Jeffrey you haven't answered my calls or texts for a week, and you wanna call me, "Boobie?" Answers Kacie.
I am so sorry, Kacie, I got into a little trouble with my kid's mother and she called the cops on me.
"Wait, hold up! What kind of trouble? What did your crazy ass do?
"Wow, K it's like that? You gonna automatically take the bitch side?"
"Dude, I've seen the maniac side of you, you forgot?"
"Nah, I didn't forget but damn, at least let me tell you what happened."
"Go ahead, I'm listening."
"Boom, so look, this psychotic chick calls my phone and tells me my daughter has a fast ass nigga over at the crib. You know I don't play when it comes to my babygirl, so I get there in 2.5 seconds. I knock on the front door hard as a motherfucker, knocked a good four times almost taking it off the hinges. My daughter finally opens the door, happy as hell to see me. I told her if she don't wipe that smile off her face I'ma do it for her; but you know I would never touch her. She staring at me all dumbfounded, so I then ask her where's this fast ass nigga? She's like, "Daddy, calm down it's just me and mommy here." So I start screaming for Latasha to get her ass downstairs. The bum bitch comes downstairs in her silk robe clapping her fucking hands, and laughing. So now I'm getting tight 'cause I don't like to play games, especially when it comes to my seeds. I told Latasha she got 2 seconds to tell me what's going on. So she like, "Damn, Jeff it sure is good to see your fine ass,"

I haven't seen her ass in almost a year. I immediately lose my cool, and grab her by the wrist yelling for her to tell me why she called me over here. She laughed in my face and said, "Nigga I called you over here so you can give me some of that good dick, and 'cause we need a little money for groceries." I turned to my daughter and told her to give me and her mom a few minutes. As soon as my daughter left the room I smacked fire out the trick.

"Huuuuuu! Jeff you didn't?!"

"Sure the fuck did, the bitch talking crazy in front of our impressionable ass daughter, and to top it all off, I saw traces of coke on her nose! In front of my daughter, Kacie?!"

"Oooh, damn, babe, I'm sorry to hear about this…so what happened next?"

"So when I smacked her she fell to the ground and started sobbing, I swear I wanted to kick the bitch in the stomach, but I just left and headed to the living room where babygirl was. Before I could reach the living room she clocks me on the top of my head with a lamp. Shit after that I just blacked and started hitting her." "Oh my, god," says Kacie.

"Our daughter runs in the room to break it up, and her mom tells her to call the cops on me! My baby is all shook up; could barely talk. Latasha jumps up from off the floor and sprints to the bathroom locking the door. I heard her on the phone with the police so I booked it, but before I could pull off in the whip them niggas caught me, man!"

"So what happened when you got to the police station?" Kacie asks.
"They had me in a holding cell for about an hour, then two detectives took me into a room to question me, and I told them exactly how it went down. The next day I went in front of a judge and pleaded my case, I'm out on bail right now." "Okay, and what type of charges are they trynna hit you with?" Asks Kacie. "Assault, and endangering the welfare of a minor." "Wow, she should be charged with endangering a child fuckin' with that coke," says Kacie. "Yeah, but I don't wanna say nothing, I need my daughter to have at least one parent around. And she is a good mother when she ain't on that shit, man."

"This whole shit just got me fucked up," Jeff sighs and says. "Damn, you really did have it rough this past week; I hope everything works out for you. And I hope you and Latasha can work on y'all issues." "I didn't even know we had an issue, I think she caught wind of me and you; she got eyes and ears everywhere." "Oh, wow, and I definitely know how salty these baby mommas can get! Lol," says Kacie. "Pssh, word, babe it's so childish tho', but forget all that when can I see you again? I've been dreaming every night of them lips of yours," Jeff says. "Mmm, you have, daddy?" "Oh, mami have I? Girl, you gave me the sloppiest, sexiest head I've ever received in my 30 years of getting head." "Lol, damn I'm poppin' like that?" Kacie asks. "Yup, everything poppin' 'bout you, babygirl, so wassup, when can I send for you? Or I can come to you." "I've been a little busy lately, but maybe in another two weeks."

"Two weeks is perfect, boo. I'll call you tomorrow, ok?" Says Jeff. "Okay, have a good day and stay out of trouble!" "I'll try, baby, later!" "Later," Kacie says and they both hang up the phone.

Oh gosh, poor Jeff.

CHAPTER 8

THE COME UP

A brief phone conversation between Dante' and his connect guy:

   "Ayo, what's good, boy it's D," says Dante'.
"Poppin', my gee?" Replies his friend, Pop.
"Everything still a go for that shit we discussed?" Dante' asks.
"Yeah, man, but yo we gotta meet up, I don't like talkin' over these phone,"
"Aight bet, where at?"
"Corner of 134 and Guy Brew," says Pop.
"Copy, on my way," says Dante' then he hangs up the phone.

Dante' pulls up to the corner of 134th avenue in his 2015 Lexus GS 350. He steps out the lavish car and gives daps to some of the dudes in front of the stores. A few moments later Pop pulls up to the block.

   "What it is, Pop?" Says Dante' giving him a dap. "Everything is everything, my dude, come to my whip so I can show you the merchandise." Dante' follows Pop to his crème colored 2016 Benz. "Woo! This you, boy?" Dante' asks him. "Yeah, man you know how I do, told you these pieces really be hitting," says Pop. "Ahh, heard you! Shit, boy I'm ready, show me what you got." Pop pulls out a handful of assorted gift cards: Macy's, Target, Bed Bath & Beyond, to name a few. "How much is on these joints?" Dante' asks. "They range from $250 to $500, that's a couple thousand all together," Pop replies. "Dope," Dante' says as he hands Pop ten crisp 100 dollar bills. "Aight, good looks, be smart with these, son," demands Pop. "You already, man thanks again, I'll holla later," responds Dante'. "One," says Pop, and the two part ways.

Dante' dials Kacie's number to update her on his progress.

   -"Hey, D," says Kacie.
- "Hey, cutie what you doing?" He asks.
-"Just got off the phone with my mom,"
-"Oh okay, well, I got them cards, you gon help me move them?"
- "Lol, definitely not!"
-"Wowww, you gon' act like that, huh?"
-"Sure am, I ain't going down with yo black ass."
-"Yeah, yeah whatever, man I'ma just have to do it myself," Dante' says shaking his head.
-"Exactly, now go make mami some money!"
-"Lmao, later, girl."
-"Later," Kacie says then she ends the call.

A few minutes later Dante' gives Pat, his baby mother a call.

   -"Yo, Pat wassup boo?" Dante' says.
-"Nothing, nigga what you want?" Pat asks him.
-"Damn, why you always so rough with me?!"
-"'Cause you ain't shit, and won't ever be shit."
-"Wow, chill out with all that shorty."
-"Nah, I ain't chillin with shit, I told you to control that Hoe of yours, she always got something slick to say."
-"Man, you still on that shit from last week, go ahead with all that petty crap.

Y'all really need to learn how to be cordial, 'cause none of y'all bitches going anywhere."
- "Smfh, if you say so, so wassup? What you callin' me for, 'cause we ain't scheduled to fuck til' Friday."
-"I got some money for you and the kids."
-"Okay, keep talking."
-"I got these gift cards that I want you to help me get off."
-"Word? Yeah I heard about this type of come up."
-"Yeah, I got em' from my mans and he is lit right now!"
-"Ok, so what I gotta do?" Pat asks.
-"I'ma drop a few off to you, and you sell some to your co-workers or fam. I know your ratchet friends love Walmart and Target."
-"Lol, and you know this. So how much is my cut?"
-"I'ma give you four cards and you can get 25% of what we make off em'. So if you sell a $500 one for $400, you get $100."
-"Hmm, I dunno, I think I need a higher percentage."
-"How, when I'm the one who put the money up?"
-"Okay, and I'm the one taking all the risk."
-"You ain't gonna be the one shopping with em', Pat."
- "I want 40%, D nothing less."
-"Okay, fine. I'm on my way over there."
-"K, bring some Henny."
-"No, I ain't fuckin' you today, I got moves to make," says Dante'.
-"Yeah sure, D see you soon," Pat says unconvinced.
-"Bye," Dante' says and hangs up the phone.

CHAPTER 9

"YOU BETTER CALL TYRONE"

"Ring! Ring! Ring!"
Kacie's phone goes off.

-"Heyyyy, Ty," Kacie says answering the phone.
-"Hey, Kacie how are you feeling today?" Tyrone
asks.
-"I'm doing okay, Hun. I actually have an interview
today at 1pm with a magazine company."
-"Wow, good for you, I hope you get the job."
-"Yes, me too, I feel so useless without a job."
-"You know you could never be useless, Kacie you're
too precious and pure for that."
-"Oh stop, I'm not a saint like you think, Ty."
-"I find that hard to believe. But, anyways I'm calling
you because I would love to take you out this
weekend, if you're available?"
-"Awww, you would? That'll be sweet, where are we
going?"
-"A friend told me about a strip of restaurants and
bars in Long Island, the place is called, The Nautical
Mile."
"Oh, wow, I've always wanted to go there, I heard it's
beautiful."
-"I'm sure not as beautiful as you, but yes, I heard it
was beautiful too. So, how about 7pm on Saturday?
-Okay, Ty that sounds like a plan. Hey, you think you
could give me a ride to my interview?"
-"Sure I can, what time should I be to you?" He asks
smiling thru the receiver.
 -"12 o'clock would be perfect," responds Kacie.
-"Okay, see you then, gorgeous, bye."
-"Bye, Ty," Kacie says and hangs up the phone.

Now that's what I'm talking about, a real gentleman.

Kacie has about an hour before Tyrone comes to take her for her interview, so she irons her business attire and flat irons her hair.

   "Knock! Knock! Knock!" Kacie hears three hard knocks at her front door.
"Who is it? She asks as she approaches the door.
"Girl, it's me! Hurry up and let me in!" Shouts Chelsea.

Kacie opens the door hastily.

   "What's the matter, Chels?" She asks.
"K, it's Dante',"
"Bitch, what happened to him? Talk!" She screams with a petrified look on her face.
"Girl, big Trey called me and told me he got locked up this morning."
"What?! That stupid motherfucker and them dumb as gift cards, man."
-"Wow, that's crazy!" Says Chelsea shaking her head.
"Wtf, I was just getting ready to go to a job interview, I'm so mad right now."
"Nah, girl you gotta reschedule that, you ain't in the right mind frame."
"I will, right now," Kacie says grabbing her cellphone.

Kacie calls the HR department and speaks to the hiring manager, Michelle Gomez.

   -"Hi, Mrs. Gomez, this is Ms. Kacie Fuller, I have an interview today with your company," Kacie says.
-"Hi, Ms. Fuller, yes, how are you today?"

-"Not so good, that's why I'm calling; may I reschedule my interview for Monday?"

-"What's wrong, is everything ok?"

-"My fiancé was in a serious car accident, I'm heading to the hospital now."

-"Oh, my I am so sorry to hear that, take as many days as you need, Ms. Fuller."

-"Thank you for being so understanding; I will call you guys with updates."

-"Okay, Ms. Fuller, again I am so sorry."

-"Thank you, Mrs. Gomez, have a nice day."

-"Goodbye," says Mrs. Gomez and they hang up the phone.

"Damn, you're a good liar, K," says Chelsea.
"Girl, only when it's absolutely necessary."
"I feel you, so what now?"
"I dunno, I guess just wait for D to call me."
"Yeah, I'm sorry, sis I know how you feel about that crazy man."
"Yes, Chels, 'cause you've been there from the start."
"And I will always be there for you, I love you, boo."
"I love you more. Are you staying with me?" Kacie asks. "No, sorry I can't, gotta pick Trey up from school soon." "Oh okay, give him hugs and kisses for me." "I will, baby later," Chelsea says as she hugs Kacie closely. "Later," Kacie replies seeing Chelsea out.

After Chelsea leaves Kacie calls Tyrone back.

-"Yo, Ty you would not believe what happened!" Kacies screams into the phone.

-"Slow down, Kacie, what's going on?" Tyrone asks.

-"This stupid ass nigga of mine got locked up!"

-"Oh, damn sorry to hear that."

-"Shit, I'm not; you do something stupid, you pay the consequences."

-"I mean that is true, but I know you care about him so you wish he wasn't in this situation."

-"Yeah, I know, I'm just talking shit 'cause I'm ticked off."

-"Well is there anything I can do to make you feel better?"

-"I dunno, I was just callin' you so you wouldn't waste your time coming here because I had to reschedule my interview."

-"Oh ok, well you know I'm still available if you need some company."

-"That actually sounds pretty comforting, how 'bout you come over with my favorite ice cream? Lol."

-"Lol, I can do that, from Cold Stone, right?"

-"Yup, glad someone remembered, and you know what surprise me on the flavor."

-"Ok, cool, I know just what to get you to cheer you up. See you in about fourty-five."

-"Ok, Hun see you," Kacie says as she hangs up the phone.

Tyrone drives his minivan to the Cold Stone on Union Turnpike in Flushing. He orders Kacie and himself The Founder's Favorite flavor in a chocolate dipped waffle cup. Tyrone hurries his way to Kacie's apartment before the ice cream melts all over his van. He reaches to her building and searches for parking. After finding a spot behind her building he then rings her intercom.

"Hey, Kacie it's me, what's the floor and apartment number?" Tyrone asks. "Fourth floor, apt 12P as in Peter," she answers as she buzzes him in.

Tyrone enters the elevator and rides it up with another tenant that's going to the same floor. "Have a nice day, ma'am!" He says as he exits the elevator. "Same to you, wow, a man with etiquette, that's uncommon these days," the woman says. Tyrone smirks, "Oh why thank you, I was surely brought up with great manners," he says as the door closes.

With Kacie's apartment door already ajar, she calls out his name. Tyrone greets her with a big smile and kiss on the cheek.

"Come on in, love, thank you for taking the time out to comfort me," Kacie says. "Girl, you know I'll always be there for you," replies Tyrone. "This I know, and can definitely feel that you have my best interest, unlike some other people I know." Tyrone smiles nice and big showing his pearly whites. "Hey, so let's dig into this ice cream before it melts, Hun," he says. "Oh, yes, yum let me see if you got some good taste!" "Lol, okay, watch, you're gonna be hooked." Kacie takes a small scoop of the ice cream. "Oh my, god! Now this is to die for!" She yells. "Seeee, I told you, you would love it, sweetie," he says as he wipes the tiny drop of ice cream off her chin. "Oh, thanks, Ty. You better dig into yours before I do, lol." They both laugh and take a seat on her brown leather couch.

After hanging out on the couch for a half an hour talking about the whole Dante' issue, Tyrone asks to use the bathroom. "Oh, it's down the hall on your right," she says while pointing in the direction of the restroom. While Tyrone utilizes the bathroom Kacie makes her way to her bar, and grabs a bottle of Mango Ciroc. Tyrone takes a seat back on the couch and notices the alcohol on the coffee table.

"Oh, wow that's a big bottle of Ciroc you got there," he says to Kacie. "Boy, this ain't even the biggest one they have, lol, do you even drink?" She asks. "Occasionally, I've never had this flavor before only the coconut one, hope it's good." Kacie grabs two glasses from the cabinet; dropping 2 ice cubes in each. She places coasters on the table before she puts the glasses down. "Oops, I forgot to grab the mango juice from the fridge, I'll be right back," she says. "Mmm, mango on mango, that sounds damn good." "Yeah, it's a banging combo, now you just watch, lol," says Kacie proudly.

Kacie likes to think of herself as a master mixologist so she takes it upon herself to pour Tyrone's "'poison." "Yikes, not too strong, Kacie I do have to drive," he says. "Ciroc is not that strong, boo don't worry," Kacie proclaims. Tyrone takes a big gulp of his drink. "Woo! Wow, that's tasty and very smooth." "Mmm, yes, yes I love it!" Kacie says as she takes a gulp from hers.

Kacie thought it would be a good idea to play a drinking game called, never have I ever. The rules of this game are for a person to start off saying, "Never have I ever," and if anyone who at some point in their lives has done the act that the person says, they must take a shot. A little terrified Tyrone asks Kacie to kick it off, so she does. After a good 10 questions go by, Kacie is drunk out of her mind and Tyrone is only a little buzzed.

"Hey, you!" Kacie yells out. "Kacie I'm right here you don't have to shout, sweetie," Tyrone says. "I'm not shouting, crazy you are!" She yells. "Okay, okay I'm sorry; I'll keep my voice down." "Good! You'll wake my neighbors," she says pointing in his face. "It's still early, babygirl no one is sleeping at this time. Are you hungry? Let's order something." "Ooh, yeah, let's order some Chinese food!" She says excitedly.

Kacie instructs Tyrone to get the menu from a draw in the kitchen. Tyrone scans the menu to see what he has a taste for. "Hurry up, Ty 'cause I already know what I want," Kacie blurts out. Tyrone goes to dial the Chinese restaurant's number, but another call comes thru first. Only ringing once, Kacie immediately snatches it from Tyrone's hand to see who's calling. The number was unfamiliar to her starting with a 718-670 so she eagerly picked it up.

-"Hello," She says.
-"Baby!" Says Dante'
"Oh my, god, Dante' baby are you okay? Did they hurt you?"
-"I'm good, boo you know that. I'm just waiting to see the judge in the morning. What you up to?"
"Nothing much, a little lonely, and I'm about to order some Chinese food."
"Your ass been drinking, huh?"

"Yeah, just a little Ciroc, probably go right to sleep after the food, you know how I do."
-"Yeah, I know you always get the itis, lol damn I'm missing you already!"
-"I miss you too, even though I'm mad at you, but we'll touch on that soon."
-"Oh boy, okay, listen they signaling for me to hang up, I love you, babe."
-"Love you too, D Later," she says and hangs up the phone.

"Thanks for not making any noise, Ty," Kacie says. "No problem, I would never want you to get in trouble with your guy, even tho' I know he doesn't deserve you." "Aww, you're so sweet, and yeah, I know that boy has put me thru enough bullshit." "So you wanna still get the Chinese food?" He asks Kacie. "Yes, of course, my mouth is watering for some Shrimp and Broccoli."

Kacie dials the Chinese restaurant's number and orders her shrimp and broccoli with a crispy egg roll, and reads off Tyrone's order that he wrote on a napkin: bbq boneless spare ribs with pork fried rice and a grape soda. The food arrives in 20 minutes and they both waste no time devouring their meals.

"Damn, now that was some good pork," says Tyrone. "Lol, yeah it looked good, my shrimp was good as well. Ty, thank you for coming over here and keeping me in good spirits, you are amazing." "It was my pleasure, and I was really looking forward to our date Saturday, but I know you have a lot going on." "Yeah, but we can definitely reschedule, maybe like next weekend." Tyrone collects their empty dishes and throws it in the kitchen garbage. "Okay, just let me know," says Tyrone. "Such a gentleman, I wish I could keep you, lol," says Kacie. "Lol, ah, that would be a dream come true for me, Kacie," he says. Kacie walks over to Tyrone and plants a soft kiss on his full lips. Tyrone grabs her by the waist and pulls her closer and kisses her back, adding tongue. "Wow, you're a great kisser, Ty," she says holding her lips. "Me? No, gorgeous your lips tasted sweeter than a strawberry, and softer than what I would imagine a cloud to be." "A poet, are we? A true Prince Charming," she says. "For you I'll be anything." "Wow, I didn't know you were this smooth, babe, I gotta watch out for you." "Lol, I'm gonna head out now, my Love, I hope to see you soon." "Aww, okay, Ty I'll call you later." "I'll be waiting!" He says as he leaves Kacie's apartment.

CHAPTER 10

THE LAST
STRAW!

Kacie attends Dante's hearing to find out the outcome of his case. Dante' stands before the judge and pleads not guilty of the crime. He claims that he did not know the gift cards were stolen, and that they were given to him as a gift. Dante's record was rather clean except for an assault charge ten years ago. The judge found him not guilty, but did warn him to stay out of trouble for the next year or there would be consequences to face. Dante', however, was charged a fine of $2,000. He smiles graciously and thanks the judge as the hearing came to a close.

"Hey, babe I have to get my release papers and then I'm all yours," he informs Kacie.
"Okay, Hun I'll be outside," she responds.

Dante' is released and meets Kacie at the front of the building.

"Damn, babe where's Chelsea, how we getting home?" He asks. "She couldn't make it; I figure we just get a cab." "You still using cabs? Nah, I'm a call for an UBER," he says. "What is an UBER, babe?" "It's an app for quick rides, damn, girl where you been?" "Lol, who knows, boy but okay cool!"

The UBER arrives in just a few minutes, and takes the two to Kacie's apartment in Jamaica, Queens.

"Ahh, man I need a shower badly!" Dante' says as he sniffs his underarms.
"Eww, yes you do; desperately, don't even sit down 'til you do." "Lol, damn it's like that?" He asks Kacie.

"Lol, oh yeah, it's like that!"
"Aight, well put something on to eat, you know a nigga starving, and I'ma hop in the shower now; I'm smelling like the bookings and shit."
"Got you, babe," says Kacie.

Kacie bakes some chicken, and makes yellow rice, broccoli and sweet plantains.

"Mmm, it's smelling good in there," Dante' yells from her bedroom. "Yup, I'm making something easy and delicious 'cause I know you ain't eat that nasty shit they was giving y'all in there." "Word, babe you know I'm funny with a lot of people's cooking, especially a filthy place like that," says Dante'.

While the food is cooking Kacie removes her clothes and makes her way into the bathroom to surprise Dante'.

"Hey, baby, mind if I join?" Kacie asks in a sexy voice. "Shit, you know I never mind," he says as helps her into the bathtub. Kacie wastes no time showing Dante' what he's been missing. She carefully drops to her knees and kisses his elongated penis.

"Ooh, damn I love it when you do that," Dante' says. Kacie now begins to lick and suck his manhood, and gently massages his balls in her hand. Dante' helps her up and turns her around so her ass would level with his dick. He slips it in her dripping pussy and begins to bang her hard.

"Oh, shit! Damn you gon' just beat it up like that, daddy?" Asks Kacie.
"Mmhm! I sure am 'cause I heard you been a bad little girl," he answers. Dante' fucks her harder and harder each time she moans.

"I'm 'bout to cum, I'm 'bout to cum!" He yells.
"Ohh! Me too, baby!" She also yells.
They both cum as Dante' pulls out of Kacie's pussy and cums on her butt cheeks. Kacie washes off and exits the tub, leaving Dante' to finish his shower. Dante' finishes up in the bathroom and put on his comfortable house clothes and slippers.

"You couldn't wait to get nice and comfy, huh? Kacie asks. "Lol, you already know!" Dante' says taking a bite of the chicken. "Really, Dante', you still doing that bullshit with your phone?" "Yo, what are you talking about now?! "You know what the fuck I'm talkin' about! Flipping your phone over like you got something to hide," yells Kacie. "Man, go ahead with all that petty shit, is just a force of habit." "Ok, fine, if that's what you say." "Kacie takes a seat at the dining table and begins to eat her food. "Damn, I gotta take a shit already, you put something in my food?" He asks jokingly. "Nope, but I should have," she responds. Dante' leaves the table and puts his phone on the charger in the bedroom then goes into the bathroom.

Kacie goes into the bedroom a few minutes later, unlocks Dante's phone and starts snooping thru it. Enraged at what she found she busts thru the bathroom door.

"Yo, wtf?!" Dante' yells.
"Son, what the fuck is Tonya doing calling and texting you? And she talkin' 'bout her and the twins miss you. Nigga, what's going on?" She demands.
"Ah, man," he quietly says.
"What?! Yo speak up!" She yells.
"Listen, man it happened a few years ago, I was drunk and horny." Kacie's face turns fiery red.
"Wait, are you telling me those twins are yours?" She asks him. Dante' looks up at her from the toilet with an ashamed look on his face.
"Yeah, Kacie they're mine," he replied.
"O.m.f.g! You fuckin' dog! She was my friend you asshole!" "Yo, I know we were wrong for that, I'm so sorry, but what's done is done, Kacie."
"You got some fuckin' nerve, and when the hell were y'all planning on telling me this, when they fuckin' turn 18?" Kacie storms away and locks herself in the bedroom.

"Fuck!" Dante' yells as he finishes up in the bathroom.

He starts to bang on the bedroom door.

"Babe, please let me in, let's talk about this," he asks Kacie.

Kacie doesn't answer, instead she texts Tonya from Dante's phone inviting her over.

Believing that it's Dante' texting her, she asks if she should bring the twins, but Kacie texts, "No, just you."

Kacie finally comes out after being locked in the room for nearly 30 minutes.

"Damn, baby it's about time," Dante' says to her. Kacie gives him a cruel look and heads to the door.

"Yo, where you going?" He asks.
"Oh, nowhere," she says as she opens the door.

Standing outside of the apartment is Tonya with her jaw opened wide. Kacie snatches her into the apartment by her shirt, and slams the door. Without asking any questions Kacie begins to pounce on her.

"Oh, my God!" Tonya yells as she attempts to guard her face. Dante' runs to break up the fight.
"K, you bugging out right now!" Shouts Dante'.
Kacie gets one last punch in before being picked up by a much stronger Dante'.

"Okay, okay so I take it you know, Kacie," Tonya says holding her bloody nose. "You damn right I know you sneaky, dirty ass bitch!" Kacie screams.
"Listen, what happened between us shouldn't have happened, but I don't regret having my babies. He might not be the best nigga to you, but he takes care of them kids," says Tonya. "But out of all the dick in the world, why'd you have to go and fuck my man? And the craziest part of it all is that I was pregnant the same time you were, but due to stress I had a miscarriage."

"I remember, and I felt so, so bad, but I couldn't abort my babies. I told Dante' that he didn't have to be a part of their lives, but he insisted, and honestly I'm glad he did," says Tonya. "Are y'all still fucking now?" Kacie asks. Tonya hangs her head. "Yes, that's why I haven't been calling you to hang out in a long time; it just doesn't feel right being around you," she says. "Wow, just wow. This is definitely my last straw with you Dante', I'm cutting both y'all scumbags off, and bitch, you can have the nigga!" Says Kacie.

Dante' breathes heavily, but remains silent.
Tonya tries again to apologize to Kacie, but she's had enough and tells her to leave. Without hesitation Tonya sees her way out.

Kacie goes into her room, rapidly packs her suite case, and calls Chelsea.

-"Chels, please tell me you're not busy?" Kacie asks.
-"No, just doing some laundry, what's up?" She asks.
-"I need you to come get me, ASAP!"
-"Girl, what happened? Where are you?"
-"Chels, just come get me out this house, I'll fill you in when I see you, smfh!"
-"Oh, boy okay I'll be there in 10."
-"Thanks, girl," Kacie says and hangs up the phone.

Dante' grabs Kacie's suite case and begs her not to leave.

"Dante' do not fuck with me! Give me my shit, now!" She yells swinging her fist at his face.

"Whoa! Chill baby! We can work this out," Dante'
pleads as he drops her suite case to the ground.
"Not in your wildest dreams, now give me my fucking
keys." "K, don't do this, I need you," Dante' says
handing her his copy of the keys. "I want you gone
when I get back," Kacie says.

Still irate Kacie leaves the apartment slamming the
door behind her. Kacie starts to cry in the elevator on
the ride down, but she quickly wipes away her tears
with the sleeve of her shirt.

"Kacie! Over here!" She hears Chelsea say.
Kacie hops into her vehicle.

"Hey, girl just drive, I wanna get as far away from
here as possible," says Kacie. "Okay, but is
everything alright?" Chelsea asks. "No, no it isn't, I
just find out some real crazy shit, Chels," Kacie says
shivering. "Oh, my god, girl you're shaking...look at
you." "Son, this nigga Dante' and Tonya been fucking
each other behind my back." "Huu! No, bitch!"
Chelsea says cupping her hands on her mouth in
shock. "No lie, girl, and guess what the craziest part
is?" "What?!" Chelsea asks. "Them twin girls," Kacie
says pausing. "Nah!" Shouts Chelsea.
"Yup! They're his." "No—fucking—way, wow I'm so
sorry, babe." "Nah, I'm not, this gave me the extra
push to get away from his dog ass." "I hope so girl
'cause you've been saying this for years now."
"I know I have, but I'm certain this time, Chels."
"Ok, babe so you gonna stay with me for a few days?"

"I'ma stay tonight, but I'm gonna call my friend Jeff from Chicago and see if he'll come out here and keep me company." "That would be dope," Chelsea says nodding her head in agreement. "Let's stop at the liquor store before we go upstairs," says Kacie. "Girl, we straight I already got some Patron upstairs." "Owww! Shit, I feel better already, lol!" "Lol, you stupid girl," says Chelsea.

The ladies arrive at Chelsea's apartment.

"Chelsea, where's Trey?"
"Oh, he's staying with his dad for a few days."
"Aww, okay, welp just us girls."
"Yup, let's order something to eat, you want pizza?" Chelsea asks. "Yeah, let's do Domino's; I can go for a chicken alfredo pasta bowl." "Lol, fat ass…yeah I want some wings, and pepperoni and bacon pizza." "Lol, okay sounds good, you order the food and I'll make the drinks." "You swear you a bartender, K." "Ha ha, don't hate 'cause I got the magic touch," Kacie says sticking her tongue out at Chelsea. "I'm glad you're in a better mood, but you know I'ma need more details, girl." "Yeah, I got you, let me just get some drinks in first." "Of course, girl," says Chelsea.

Kacie goes into Trey's room and dials Jeff's number.

-"Well, look who it is," says Jeff.
-"Lol, yes, it's meee. What you doing?" Kacie asks.
-"I'm home just finished cooking myself some jerk chicken, rice and peas and mixed vegetables."
-"Damn, that sounds good, I didn't know you were a gourmet chef."

-"Lol, there's still a few things you don't know about me yet."

-"I bet, babe. I'm calling you 'cause I'm ready for you to come out here," says Kacie.

-"Oh, really, you are?"

-"Yes, I want us to spend the weekend together."

-"What about your dude?"

-"I left that nigga! He's a total dick."

-"Wow, something serious must have happened between y'all."

-"Oh, yeah it's serious, something unforgivable, but I'ma tell you all about it when I see you."

-"Damn, I gotta wait to hear the juice, or tea as you would say."

-"Lol, yes you gotta wait. So are you gonna come?" She asks.

-"Of course I will, I told you I miss you like crazy. Send me the link for the hotel and I'll book it."

-"Yay! Okay, babe can't wait to see you again."

-"Me too, sexy...what's your size? I'll pick you up some lingerie."

-"Mmm, I love a man that knows how to spoil a girl, lol. You can get me a large, and get some role play stuff."

-"Lol, kinky, I like."

-"Yes, very, but let me get back to my home girl."

-"Okay, y'all have a goodnight, don't forget to send me the hotel link."

-"I won't, boo, goodnight," says Kacie and she ends the call.

Kacie returns back to the living room where Chelsea is.

"Sooo, what he say, girl?" Chelsea asks.
"Ayyye! He's coming out here this weekend, and he's paying for the hotel!" "Listen! Now, that's what I'm talking 'bout!" Chelsea says giving Kacie a high five. A few minutes later the doorbell rings.

"Who is it?" Chelsea asks.
"It's Domino's," a soft voice answers.
Chelsea opens the door and collects the food tipping the young man $5.

"K, I want to meet this Mr. Jeff, 'cause he has to get your best friend's approval." "Ha ha, okay, girl, even tho we ain't listen to each other about Dante' and Trey, lol." "That's a fact, girl, but hey, we was young and dumb, now we some grown, smart, fine ass women," says Chelsea. "Right, honestly, me and Tyrone have been talking and hanging out a lot lately." "Tyrone has always been a cutie, but he don't make enough money for me." "Lol, that's why he ain't for you, everyone ain't a big drug dealer like your baby father." "Yeah, that's true, the other day he gave me two grand to put into Trey's college fund, and gave me some money for my bills." "Yeah, y'all might not have worked out, but he's a great provider, and I know my god baby adores him."

Kacie and Chelsea are on their third cup of Patron, and just finished up eating their delicious Domino's.

"Ugh, this nigga D done called me phone about 40 times, like dude face it, you fucked up to the point of no return," says Kacie.

"He is a bozo for real, like c'mon out of all the pussy in the world, you choose your girl's friend? He know not to ever step to me 'cause I'll kick him right in his balls." Kacie gives Chelsea a high five. "Lol, and that's why you and I are sisters. Word to me, every time I see Tonya I'm gonna beat her stank ass." "I feel you, girl and the fact that you use to change them babies' diapers gotta be extra crazy." "Man, is it, pretty little girls too, now if I see them I'll probably just break down and cry." "Aww, you're gonna have your own little family one day, babe, the timing and the dude is just wrong." "You speaking some real shit, Chels, thanks for always keeping it a hundred with me." "Heyy, you gotta repay loyalty with loyalty, nothing less.

The girls continue their girl talk for another hour, sipping their Patron and taking shots. Dante' kept calling Kacie, but she stuck to her word of ignoring him, and fell asleep around midnight.

CHAPTER 11

YOU CAN ONLY
CHOOSE ONE

-"Hey, baby! I just landed in the Big Apple!" Jeff says to Kacie via phone.

-"Yay! Welcome to my city, can't believe it took lil' ole me to get you in NY, lol, you on your way to pick up your rental car?" Kacie asks.

-"Sure am, you know I gotta ride in style and show y'all NY cats how Chi-town get down."

-"Ha ha, I hear that, talk that talk, baby. Well hit me when you're on your way, I have someone that wants to meet you."

-"The famous Chelsea, huh?

-"You guessed right! Yeah she said you have to get her approval before we move forward, lol."

-"Is that right? Well I'm confident that'll I'll win her vote."

-"I am too, okay Jeff I'll see you when you get here."

-"Ok, babe, Later," Jeff says and he hangs up the phone.

Jeff fills out the paperwork for his rental car, a silver BMW 2 series. Jeff is adamant about riding in style any and everywhere he goes. It didn't take long for Jeff to reach Chelsea's apartment, once there he called Kacie to meet him downstairs.

Kacie comes downstairs in a sexy, tight fitting peach colored dress, and some Michael Kors sandals.

"Sheesh, you out here looking like a freshly picked peach," he says then kisses her on the lips, "Taste like one too," he added. Kacie blushes and hugs him securely. "Babbby! I missed you," says Kacie. "Well I'm here now, girl, how 'bout you show me just how much you have?" He says squeezing her ass cheeks. "Lol, not out here, boy come on let's go introduce you to my bestie." Kacie grabs his hand and they walk into Chelsea's building.

"Chelsea! Jeff's here!" Kacie shouts as they enter the apartment. Chelsea comes from out of her room to meet him.

"Hi, Jeff I'm Chelsea, nice to meet you," she says shaking his hand. "It's a pleasure to meet you, dear," he replies. "So, what are your intentions with my sister?" "Lol, man you don't waste no time."
"Oh, gosh, she sure doesn't," says Kacie.
"That's right, I'm tired of my girl getting played, so I gotta check em' at the door." "Well, Chelsea, I'm a totally different breed than what she's used to, I'm a real man, all day every day." "Heard it all before," both Chelsea and Kacie say, being that it's one of their favorite slogans. "Oh, that's foul, y'all just gon' double team me like that?" "Lol, yup, I told you together we're a force to be reckoned with." "Hey, guys how about we finish this conversation over lunch?" Jeff asks. Kacie and Chelsea look at each other. "Okay, sure, we're always down for some good food," says Chelsea. "Truuue," Kacie adds in.

The trio decides to go to, "Chili's Grill & Bar" in Glendale, Queens.

"Babe, you wanna drive since it's your town?" He asks Kacie. "Hehe, oh, you don't know? Only thing Kacie knows how to drive is someone insane," Chelsea says laughing. "Not funny, Chels!" Kacie says shoving her. "Damn, babe you 31 and don't know how to drive?" "I'm 32, and nope I don't, I never got around to learning," she says. "Boo, that's sad, we gotta teach you, ASAP," Jeff says as he types the restaurant's address in the GPS. "Okay, I'm ready whenever you are," says Kacie. "It says we'll be there in 30 minutes, does that sound about right?" He asks. "Yeah, it does," says Chelsea.

In exactly 30 minutes they reach at the restaurant, and are seated in a nice booth. After looking over their menus, they place an order for drinks first.

"Now, Jeff I hope we don't have a reoccurrence of what happened the last time we went out to eat," Kacie says. "We won't, baby I don't know what got into me that night." Chelsea widens her eyes and says, "Yes, Jeff I heard all about your temper tantrum." "Dang, girl you blew me up to your home girl?" "Of course, ain't that what friends are for, lol, but yeah seriously, I'm watching you." "Don't watch too hard, I might flash you, lol." "Lol, now that I wouldn't mind." "Ha ha, y'all are too cute. Damn them drinks should've been here by now," says Chelsea.

A few minutes later their drinks come out, and they put their entrée order in with the waiter.

"So, Jeff what do you do for work?" Asks Chelsea. "I'm actually a retired fire fighter," he answers. "Wow, lucky," she says. "I put a lot of hard years in, and now I'm enjoying the fruits of my labor. What do you do?" "I'm an active, postal worker, been there almost ten years." "Nice," he says. "Thanks, how many kids, and baby mommas do you have?" "Lol, I didn't know this was an interview, but I have five kids, three baby mothers." "Ouch, that's a lot of baby mommas." "Chels, stop, leave Jeff alone." "I'm just saying, I hope he ain't trynna make you the fourth." "Nope, I'm trynna make her my wife!" "Umm, Jeff I don't think we're there, yet," says Kacie. "Oh, but we're gonna get there, baby trust." "Lol, oh Jeff," Kacie says fanning him off.

Chelsea leans over and whisper to Kacie, "Girl I don't think he's playing, you better be careful with psycho over there." "Ah, c'mon no secrets at the table, guys," Jeff says. "Sorry, Hun. Mmm here comes the food," says Kacie.

The crew is satisfied with their meals and orders one more round of drinks.

"Make them stronger, please!" Kacie shouts to the waiter. "Shhh, girl you sound like a lush," Chelsea tells Kacie kneeing her in the leg. "You know I'm going thru it right now, boo, and I'm in need of something strong." "I'm gonna take your mind off of that clown tonight, okay, babe," says Jeff. "Okay," says Kacie as she grabs Jeff's face and kisses him uncontrollably.

"Get a room!" The guy at the next table shouts. "Fuck you, buddy! Mind your business!" Jeff yells back. "Sorry, Jeff it's my fault, please pay him no mind," says Kacie. "You wanna take this outside, pussy?!" The guy yells. "Ha ha, I don't think that's what you really want," Jeff says now standing up. "Kacie get your man! Try to calm him down," says Chelsea. "Jeff, Jeff come on it's not worth it," Kacie says as she tugs on his sleeve. "You're right let's just go," Jeff says.

Jeff pays the bill and the three walk toward the exit.

"That's what I thought! You better bounce!" The man yells out. Jeff speed walks towards the man and spits directly into his face.

"Ohhh!" Another customer shouts.

The two begin to exchange punches. The manager comes out to see what the commotion is all about. Kacie and Chelsea finally are able to pull Jeff off of the man and rush him outside.

"Yo! You're a wild boy!" Says Chelsea. "See, I told you his temper is crazy," says Kacie. Jeff breathes heavily, but remaining quiet with his fists clinched tightly. "You want me to drive, Jeff?" Chelsea asks him. He nodes yes, and they get in the car.

Chelsea drives to her apartment and tells Kacie to come with her upstairs for her belongings.

"Girl, the way that man lost his cool like that, something ain't right," says Chelsea. "Damn, Chels, I said that same thing to myself. But I do like him." "I think he's a cool brother, but his temper is scary, Kacie, are you okay with going to the hotel with him?" "Yeah, girl I'll be fine, I'ma text you the hotel we'll be at, just in case." "Yes, you better," she says hugging Kacie. "Love you, girl," says Kacie.
"Love you too," Chelsea says rolling Kacie her suite case. "Later," the two say as Kacie leaves the apartment.

Kacie gets back in the car with Jeff for their night ahead.

"Are you good now, Jeff?" She asks.
"Yup, just peachy," he retorts and flashes her a smile.
"Good, can we stop by my apartment first, I forgot something over there." "Sure, babe," he says.

10 minutes later they reach at Kacie's apartment.

"Aren't you gonna invite me up?" Jeff asks.
"Umm, yeah c'mon," she says waving her hand for him to follow her.

As Kacie and Jeff walk towards her building Kacie spots Dante' in the lobby.

"Oh, shit!" She says. "What?" He asks.
"Umm, nothing, you know what; I don't need to go upstairs anymore." "Why not, I thought you forgot something?" Jeff asks.

"I thought so too, but I just remembered that I used it all." "Okay," he says sounding confused.

When Kacie and Jeff began walking back to the car Dante' spots her and calls out her name.

"Kacie! Ayo, Kacie!"

Kacie ignores him and speeds up.

"Babe, who is that guy shouting your name like that?" Jeff asks. "Yo, I know you ain't bring no nigga over here," says Dante' from afar. "Wait, is that Dante'? Jeff asks. Kacie starts to tremble. "Yup, sure is, c'mon let's get back in the car," she says yanking him by the wrist. Dante' jogs to catch up to Kacie, gripping her by the arm.

"Ay, my man she don't want you know more, so beat it," Jeff says pulling Kacie away from him. Dante' snuffs Jeff in the left eye causing him to lose his balance. "No! Dante' stop!" Kacie shouts. "Nah, fuck that! I should knock your thot ass out too!" "Thot?! Nigga I'll kill you! Jeff yells out and charges at Dante'. The two wrestle and fall to the ground. Kacie yells for them to stop but they fight even harder. All of a sudden Jeff pulls out a shiny object from his ankle and jabs it into Dante's stomach.

"Ahhhh!" Dante' lets out.
"Oh my, God Jeff!" Kacie yells as she kicks the apparent knife out his hands. Kacie drops to her knees near Dante' and applies pressure to his wound.

"Jeff, get the fuck outta here! You took it to fucking far. "Kacie I'm so sorry I didn't mean to." "Goooo! Before I call the cops on your ass. I need to get to a hospital," whispers Dante'. "Somebody help!" Yells Kacie, but no one is around. Jeff finally decides to take off in his rented BMW. Kacie looks for a cab but is unsuccessful so she calls for an UBER.

A grey Infiniti pulls up 5 minutes later.
Kacie runs to the car.

   "Oh, shit, Ty! What the hell you doing driving for UBER? You know what answer that later, I need your help." Tyrone stares at Kacie. "Oh, my, Kacie are you bleeding?!" He asks. "No, it's not mine, please help me, Dante' got stabbed, he's on the ground over there," she says pointing to where he is.

Tyrone runs out of the car to Dante' and picks him up off the ground with Kacie's assistance.
They reach to Jamaica Hospital in less than 10 minutes. Dante' is brought into the emergency department and is taken in by the nurses.

Kacie paces back and forth in the waiting area.
Tyrone stays by her side and tries to keep her calm.

   "Ty, he lost a lot of blood," she says with tears rolling down her face. "You did a great job applying pressure to the stab wound, he should be okay." "How are you always at the right place at the right time?" She asks. "I just started working for UBER tonight; it's so crazy that you happened to be my second customer." Kacie smiles.

"What made you leave the taxi business and work for them?" She asks. "I heard they had more flexibility and that the tips are good, so here I am." "And I'm glad you're here. I know I tell you all the time, but thank you and I appreciate you."

The nurse comes out and let's Kacie know that Dante' will be just fine and can have visitors now.

Kacie tells Tyrone the good news and asks him to wait for her.

Dante' is pleased to see Kacie walk into his room.

"Dante', I'm so sorry about what that lunatic did to you." "K, it's okay, I'm just happy to be alive. You know I never meant to hurt you." "I don't wanna talk about that right now, D." "But, I can't go another day without you, I love you." "I love you too, but I cannot be with you." "But you're here right now, I know you still care." "Of course I do, you were the love of my life, but you've taken me for granted for way too long." "Kacie, I will change for you." "Change for yourself, that's the only way it'll be genuine and everlasting.

Kacie kisses Dante' on his forehead and waves goodbye.

"Please don't go," says Dante'.
"I left a long time ago, well at least mentally I did," Kacie says then walks out the room.

Kacie returns to Tyrone, running into his arms.
He affectionately embraces her back.

"Is he gonna be okay?" He asks.
"Yeah he will be, what you doing after work?" Kacie
asks. "I don't have anything planned, and like I said
my schedule is flexible, so I can be off right now."
"I know just the place that we can go," she says.

The two walk out the hospital hand and hand.

Kacie types in the GPS the address of the Hotel that
she and Jeff were supposed to go to.

"Where is this address to?" Tyrone asks.
"Don't worry about that, just drive, baby, just drive,"
Kacie says while winking and biting her bottom lip.

THE END...

Author Lauren "Lush" Collier

Other Books by the Author:
Genre- Poetry

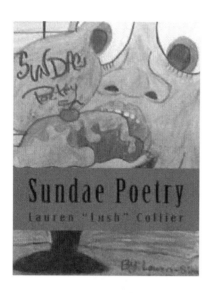

Contact Information:

Email- *Poetrybylush@yahoo.com*

Facebook- Lauren "lush" collier

Instagram- Laurenlushcollier

All feedback is welcomed!

Made in the USA
Columbia, SC
19 November 2021